The Ramblings of a Condemned Man

by Kevin Byrne

NEVER STOP NEVER QUIT
Portland, Oregon
NeverStopNeverQuit.com

Dedication

This book is dedicated to us, our loved ones, and our supporters. Thank you for the motivation every day.

This collection is published by NEVER STOP NEVER QUIT, a charitable foundation whose mission is to raise funds, support treatment, and promote awareness in the fight against multiple sclerosis. One hundred percent of the profits from this book will go toward that fight.

Because it is a fight.
For approximately 2.3 million people
with MS worldwide, the fight is not over and it
won't be over until a cure is found.

It will never stop...nor will we
It will never quit...nor will we
This is why we fight!

Never Stop... Never Quit...®
For more information, please go to: NeverStopNeverQuit.com

To donate to our efforts through Bike MS, please go to:

Main.NationalMSSociety.org/goto/EMBK

Thank you, Mom, Carly, Tommy, and Ellie: for keeping me grounded, letting me fly away, and welcoming me with open arms when I return. I love you.

Table of Contents

Chaos

I wrote this piece as a preface to try to explain my logic behind the ramblings I have included in this book. Chaos is not a perfect word choice, but it is the best explanation I can supply when I address the inevitable question, "What were you thinking?"

My life is and always has been rife with chaos. Some of the turmoil has been inflicted on me; I am merely a victim. Other times, I've been guilty of instigating disarray. There were joint efforts as well, both inflicted and self-instigated. And, of course, chaos is often a simple fact of nature. As to the correct proportions of responsibility, I don't know, although prudence would split most of the blame between nature and me.

I don't believe my body experiences a greater share of discord as compared to others. My mind, however, finds it challenging to see beyond chaos, many times to the detriment of the peace and beauty around me. Looking back on my life, the images that most readily come to mind are indeed the chaotic, the horrific, and the burdensome. Many great recollections are there, they just play second fiddle to my demons.

In and of itself, confronting chaos isn't bad. You can realize a tremendous amount of satisfaction by solving impossible challenges, overcoming overwhelming odds, or righting the wrongs around you; it is the calling of every superhero. But, when or where does it end? At what point will our hero look beyond today's villain, stop reminiscing over yesterday's evil, and forgo anticipation of tomorrow's plight?

It must be nice, taking off the cape to enjoy the day's treasures. Unfortunately, this freedom is not afforded to condemned men; my sentence is the recurring vision of chaos. The reality of my multiple sclerosis (MS) further antagonizes the turmoil that is already deep inside me. I watch the incessant thrashing my body has undertaken since 1999, when I was first diagnosed. "What's next?" rattles through my mind with its own dedicated line to every emotion and fear I possess. I am indeed a condemned man, but not for the reasons you might assume. The chaos of my MS falls mostly into the last category: it's a simple fact of nature. I'm not a victim of my disease; it's just another obstacle in life. One powerful difference with the chaos of MS is the answer to my question, "When does it end?"

It doesn't.

Writing has become my way of loosening the shackles that barrages of chaos, both MS-related and simple facts-of-life, inflict on my mind and body every day. I first started writing stories meant only for my daughter, for her to read when she ultimately receives my journals, when they become hers. In these journals (okay, fine...it's a diary), I share my thoughts, hopes, and dreams about life so that someday Ellie will have a vivid picture of the man her daddy was.

In late 2010, writing became my response to the increasing levels of chaos caused by my MS. The blogs I write are my attempt to express the hope that someday there will be an answer to "When does it end?" One piece in this book is appropriately titled *The Completely Inconsequential Ramblings of a Condemned Man*. It is adapted from a series of blog posts I wrote in 2017, documenting the damage MS has done and will continue to inflict on me. By confronting the chaos, bearing everything to my readers through the blog, I have been able to raise funds and awareness in our fight against the devastating effects of multiple sclerosis.

More importantly, the more I wrote about the chaos of my MS and shared it with others, the more my own fears lessened. The main subject of the blog series—this Kevin Byrne— now carries the weight, not the author.

If writing helped me cope with my MS, why not try writing about other aspects of my life?

In 2014, I wrote the novella *...in abeyance*. The main character, Chris Baxter, is the personification of chaos I have carried for far too long. Chris is who I am, was, wanted to be, feared, struggled to overcome, and so much more, wrapped up and scripted into an entirely fictional persona who lives in a fictional world (with a heavy smattering of historical context in this alternate reality). Placing turmoil on the shoulders of this character relaxed the burden on my own.

My revelation was earth-shattering! I wrote stories overflowing with the anxiety of my own unrest. Sometimes an entire saga addressed just one particular struggle I faced. My favorites are those based on the utter confusion in my head that I just can't quite accurately describe; the alternate fantasy world became a surrogate for the chaos I was unable to express otherwise.

Regardless of why I wrote these stories, sharing my chaos this way has helped me sleep a bit better. Maybe it discounts my fears. Maybe it validates them. However, it is my hope that the therapeutic value I get from writing pales in comparison to the enjoyment you will get from reading my tales. Time will tell.

After my most recent struggles with MS and personal chaos, a harsh campaign lasting nearly two years, I gathered some of my favorite stories and sent them to my editor. They are some of the words I wrote or revisited to help battle my own chaos. In addition to *Chaos*, *...in abeyance*, and *The Completely Inconsequential Ramblings of a Condemned Man*, I have included four short stories. My writings are indeed ramblings because I sometimes feel as if I have little control over what happens in the story.

I am merely a conduit.

Kevin

May 2018

The Introspective Ramblings of a Condemned Man

Essence

Why do you want to know who I am?

You have always yearned to define existence. It is your nature. Ever since an animal first ripened into the beast you now call humankind, the need to identify and classify has made you unique among all life.

My simpler creatures limit thought to “How?”

- “How do I satisfy my hunger?”
- “How do I keep myself safe when alarmed?”
- “How do I rest when my frame grows weary?”
- “How do I satisfy my urges when desire peaks?”

Adam also challenged, “Why?” as did all who came after him. He developed the rhetoric to question his own being and that of the world he claimed to oversee.

I am the answer to all your mysteries, the source of all information you desire. You search for my truth, but do not know why.

I understand the way all existence began for I am the essence that made it so.

Long before you came to be, my will created the universe's infinite void.

Within this space, I created galaxies and filled them with stars, each forming its own system. I gave you your Sun, your Earth, your land, your home, even the chair you now sit in while pondering questions of a higher calling. You gave everything a name, claimed ownership to all you could touch, then sought to reserve all you should see. You search for more, solely to claim.

There is much beyond that which your vision and instruments observe. In time, you will discover more than you can possibly fathom now. You will understand more about existence and the life forever beyond your grasp.

You will never approach my essence.

I don't restrain your illusions of entitlement, nor do I encourage them. They merely exist. I know how your perceptions will develop, for I know exactly what your future holds, for I alone have complete control over your progression, for I created everything. As a race, you each have free will—something I ensure your perception of. You have broken beyond the constraints of animal instinct; your decisions come from a more complex assemblage of inspirations.

You define beauty. You evaluate potential. You search for moral imperfections.

Both your greatest triumphs and most horrid atrocities come from your ability to infer, imagine, hope, and fear.

This sets you apart from all other forms of life. Thus far, you are my greatest creation.

There are many titles you have given my essence in your attempt to place human confines over the tiny sliver of that which you think is understood.

I took many forms in your ancient cultures, each defining scopes of a physical world. Your Hebrews centered me as one deity, Yahweh. I am Allah. I am God. I am described through an abundance of titles, countless in number, equal to all but one—Essence.

Your religions have pitted their Creationism against your science's Evolution.

In literature, I am the paranormal, the phenomenon. I am your Overlord.

Everything that is extends from my bestowal: your idolized history; your contemptible past; the lives you cherish, dread, and deplore today; the future you fear will never come. I know the results of your submissions and the accomplishments of your strides. I know because I have seen them, I have scripted their piece. Everything resides in sequence, throughout so many ages past and eons yet to come, all playing out in one concurrent instance, just as it has since I first created time. There is nothing you can do to change the present, for the future has already executed and the past will unfold as foretold. Time would not exist without your contribution, for each moment of time exists solely for you.

War and famine, disease and adversity—these are not trials of your resolve or your faith. They are merely elements in my timeline. The day will come when you find an end to all conditions you call suffering. You will discover. You will create effects far worse than what your mind could possibly fathom today.

I take great pleasure in all you have accomplished. What you see as pain and misfortune do not bring me sorrow, for these instances are merely unfolding as I have created them.

I need to share my account, so I have composed this time for you.

I don’t know why.

I'll Never Breathe Again

What do I think of, knowing I'll never breathe again?

Many years ago, the mere implications of this phrase forged inquietude far beyond the dull senses analogous to humans. The first time I faced the possibility that "I'll never breathe again," my body was in an environment my mind found unfamiliar and unexplored. The burning array of color defining the atoll was unmatched by anything I had ever witnessed on land. Once I was 110 feet to the sand, even those primary images lost their impact. How many shades are there on the spectrum? Colors in the sea looked like turtles had carried bright hues from the shore, growing in complexity each time they were passed off, first to the rays, then the garden eels, until finally the squid painted each vibrant splash along the coral reef.

I was lost in their splendor until somehow one of my new friends told me, "It's time to go." This was not my world, my visit limited by the gear carried on my back. It was a reminder of where I belong. But I was not yet ready to break away, to return to the ceiling of this magnificent existence. So, I stayed; I stayed until the electroception of every critter yelled, "No! You must go now." I bid their world farewell, promising to return when mine again became too much of a bore.

My extended visit was folly, for I carried with me neither the resources nor the companionship required. During my return to the surface, my supply was exhausted. In an instant, there were millions of pounds of water separating me from atmosphere. White turned to gray. Blue to brown. Soon, everything threatened to become black as my eyes begged my new friends for guidance. My ears felt them mocking, in one united chorus, the foolishness of decisions made. "Our home will not tolerate your intrusion. You are our guest for only as long as you are welcome. Nothing more."

"I'll never breathe again!" was my only thought. The krill pushed against my body, trying to reject me from their world and back to mine.

"We can't do this alone, my friend. It's up to you to fight and kick. If you want to live, kick."

I fought. To the surface I kicked, where I relished filling my lungs once again. I'll forever carry the scars of my first brush, respectfully returning to their world countless times since the day I swore, "I'll never breathe again."

That was the day I learned my idiocy will drive the day I never breathe again.

The second time I faced the possibility, my body was in an environment my mind considered exotic and unexplored. My throat was exhausted by the struggle to gasp. Nothing was there. I no longer screamed, for there was no more air with which I could make a sound.

She did that to me. My adolescence paled in comparison to her allure. I was her junior in years, her subordinate in passion. She held the prepotent title in both our public and private moments, teaching me all I would need, all I would want...

Breath was no longer an indulgence, a luxury to call for at will. When she was near, I boxed savagely for each gasp of air, for I was melted by thoughts of the consequence if she were to prevail. She struggled to take with as much passion as she fought to give. It was as if I wrestled not to claim victory, but simply to survive and enjoy the fruits of another day with my love. But she held the advantage in our first encounter, and every time after. When her lust overcame my puerility, and she claimed her prize, my mind momentarily screamed, “I’ll never breathe again.” Naturally, this did not happen.

I tried to separate my desires from fear, but that was not possible. I discovered passion is my fear. When it finally takes leave, will I never want to breathe again?

With my question answered countless times over, I realized love captures my heart with an array of enticing weapons; it holds me with the sharpest blades, yet its inevitable loss is but the tiniest of punctures. If my heart does bleed, it is healed in a wink. Loss, pain, misfortune—these are but a few of the terms you may use to describe the calamities of my life. Their damage is limited to my body and the physical world it occupies. The impact of adversity on my heart and mind is like the minuscule suffering caused by the strike of a single grain of sand blown across a beach.

As days turned to weeks and weeks to years, the sandy winds blew, capturing my legs. As the dune pushed higher and immobilized my body, I was no longer free to choose a different course. Every loss returned to remind me of my fallibility; when combined, the collective tiniest of punctures will shred a heart to pieces. Every grain of sand aspires to become a mountain. And when the agony of my recollections became too much to bear, I lifted my lumbered arms. With a pistol under my chin, I inhaled a goblet of life and, for the third time, whispered, "I'll never breathe again." If those words were to be true, I would control their course, not the fucking sand.

But the winds continued to swirl, taking with them several grains. Loved ones returned and aided strangers, their blades now used to dig my body free. Everything will change. I learned two lessons that day: everything will change, and I will breathe again.

I relished the understanding that I alone determine my fate. Since that day, every breath I've elected to take has been more wondrous than the last. They were no longer a struggle to maintain, were not a burden to endure, they were my...

They were my sovereignty–until your grasp took hold. So many questions flood my mind.

"Why did you pick me?"

"How long did you know?"

"What will you tell her?"

So, you ask me what do I think of, knowing I'll never breathe again?

The Dark Ramblings of a Condemned Man

Jimmy the Kid

He was just a kid.

I wonder if I looked that young when I made my first kill. Must've been...how many years ago? God, I can't believe it's been so long. It still feels like yesterday.

The old coot could barely move, just sitting around all day in his Barcalounger, waiting for someone to come drag him to bed when it was time to go to sleep. I just remember being so scared, slinking around the nursing home, sure I'd get caught. But I finally found his room.

He jumped as soon as he saw me barrel through the door, one ring on the end of a wire saw hanging over each index finger. I got to him before he could get up, but he still put up one hell of a fight—until I got that wire around his neck. That always slows 'em down. It took me over three minutes to cut all the way through. I almost had to stop a couple of times; the sight was making me sick, but I remembered the instructions my teacher gave me: "Make it gruesome. Send a message."

All too often, he had to correct me and clean up after my mistakes.

“Not enough blood.”

“You left a fingerprint.”

“Never draw attention to yourself.”

The normal five-kill training cycle wasn’t enough for me. I needed eight to become certified and cleared to work on my own. With Jimmy, I would’ve signed him off after his first kill and sent him on his way, if only to get some distance between us.

The kid scares me.

They assigned him to me five weeks ago, when he was fresh out of Phase 2: Screening and Aptitude. They figured I was a good fit for him because we already knew each other from before Phase 1. How the hell they usually pick ‘em is beyond me. It’s not like there’s a “Contract Killer” section in the classifieds. They sure don’t have their own booth on career day. I was born into the trade myself; a legacy. Like father, like son.

Not with Jimmy though: he tracked *them* down. Well, tracked *me* down, that is. Right after I did the Gatling job in July, this guy—Jimmy, as I later found out—walked up to me on Morris Street. I didn't know him, and he didn't know me, at least I thought he didn't. He was holding a newspaper in his hand, and just as I was getting out of my car, he stuck the front page right under my nose. "Hey!" he said. "Did you see today's paper?"

I'm sure the grainy black-and-white photograph of a bloodstained sheet covering Gatling's body sent the proper message. They probably spent a long time looking for the rest of her. That was a fun job. I just turned away from the kid.

Then, right down the street, Jimmy just blurted out, "How much did they pay you for this?" The kid blew my mind.

I mumbled something like, "Get the hell outta here with that," and went on my way. Jimmy didn't follow. He just stood there and yelled out, "Tell them I want in!" I kept walking, didn't even acknowledge he was still yelling at me. How the hell did he know?

Of course, I had to report the incident. I told them absolutely everything I knew—which was nothing. No one was around when I went into Gatling's shop that night. There was no way this kid, or anyone, could have followed me. No way at all.

They picked up Jimmy later that week for Phase 1: Identification. That's when they dig in deep to find out who you really are and how willing you are to get your hands dirty. This line of work isn't for everybody. Actually, it's not for anyone decent.

Before putting you in the program, they walk you through some gruesome past jobs, some of the messiest ones we've done, with photos and all, just to see if you can handle it. If you pass Phase 1, they set you up with a couple of mock scenarios. That's Phase 2. Usually, it's just an animal or some random homeless guy who won't be missed. They test and grade you on your strength, technique, and staying power—your ability to stomach the sight and smell. If you pass, you move on to live training exercises. If you fail, you disappear. Jimmy passed with flying colors.

He must have told them how my cover was blown, but they never mentioned it to me. I knew better than to ask Jimmy. Besides, once he's up and running, I'm retired.

His first kill was much like my own: a nobody, a random target who was of no interest to our foundation. It was just a practice kill, to see if you could execute when the rubber met the road. The objective was to stage it like a real job, and to make it gruesome, send a message.

He picked a seventy-six-year-old widow with no immediate family (closest was her niece, a fourth-grade schoolteacher). Jimmy was quiet when he broke into her home and slipped an ice pick through the base of her skull as she slept in the rocking chair. That was smart. Making it gruesome doesn't mean you have to make it difficult. Man, if I had known that on my first kill, life would've been so much easier. You can always add gruesome—after they're dead. Jimmy wasted no time proving he had both the stomach and the creativity for the job. He actually positioned Aunt Wendy's body parts on the floor to spell out the words "U DID THIS," as a message for whoever stepped foot into the blood-soaked living room.

His next test was a moving hit. Jimmy waited for me to radio in the target from his hide site, seven hundred feet from the freeway. "Motorcycle. Red helmet. Southbound. Go." I timed my call so he would have about ten seconds before the mark passed from his field of view.

Jimmy did it in four. I wasn't sure how to take it when I heard him say, "Watch the hands." Well, not until I saw the pigeon careen back, sending both him and his bike sprawling across the road at sixty-five miles an hour. Jimmy hit the bastard on his right hand. If the shot didn't kill him, the spectacular crash would. Of course, the freight truck jackknifing over the top of the poor bastard was just icing on the cake. Figuring he had earned a bit of praise, I radioed, "Good one, kid. Where'd you learn to shoot like that?"

"I'm not a kid," was his only reply. Asshole. He was probably an arcade nerd growing up. Shoot-em-up games, that's my guess.

The third test was multiple targets. I gave Jimmy the names: Mr. and Mrs. Andrew Vines of Oakdale Retirement Community. The rest was up to him, but he had to complete the assignment by nine o'clock that night, and it was five thirty in the afternoon when the clock started. The Vines lived in a secure high-rise apartment forty-five minutes away.

The kid didn't even blink an eye; he just walked out the door.

At 8:35 p.m., Jimmy came strolling back in. His pants were ripped at the knee and up the side. "Mission accomplished?" I asked.

"Mission accomplished," he snickered.

"How did you get in the building?"

"Easy," he said. "I tore my jeans, then told some old lady I crashed my bike and had somehow lost my keys. She bought it and let me in. No questions asked other than, 'Are you okay, Sonny?'" I complimented him on the trick, but Jimmy just dismissed my words.

"And how did you get into the target's apartment?"

Jimmy smiled and shrugged his shoulders. "I just told them I couldn't find the family I was looking for. People always want to help a stranger in need, I guess. I can look pretty sappy if I have to."

I shuddered as I asked the next question. "Did you make it gruesome?" The kid didn't say a word and just handed me a plastic bag. Inside were three fingers, an ear, and four little bloodied disks. "What are these?" They almost looked like seashells.

"Kneecaps!" he boasted with a haunting smile. "It'll have the cops racking their brains for weeks trying to figure out the motive for this one." The kid really scares me. I mean, who the hell thinks of that shit, especially someone so new to this kind of work?

To join the organization, you have to prove your willingness to sacrifice anything. Number four was a test of Jimmy's dedication. "How long have you lived in Bakers?" I asked, easing into the task.

"All my life," Jimmy replied with an air of indifference. "In fact, I live just a few miles from the house I was born in. There's not much here, but what the hell. I figured I'd stay until a better opportunity comes along. One boring place is as good as another, I guess."

I followed up with, "Do you have any close relationships?" He looked down, squirming uncomfortably as he rubbed a pattern on the rug with his foot.

"Not really. I tend to keep to myself. Sure, I'm friendly with the people I'm around. It seems like every year or so, I drift away and hook up with new mates. I never really break up with the old ones...they just go away and spend their time with other guys." I could see Jimmy's discomfort. His social life was a strain; it's probably what brought him to us in the first place. Sometimes, a man finds living a barbarian's life in the shadows is preferred to blending in to normalcy alongside every other cog.

Then I sharpened my focus. "What's your longest relationship?" Jimmy's eyes lit up like the lifeless wooden doll who had just taken his first breath, infused with the spirit of a fairy princess.

"Sue Ellen Kapict," he cooed. "I've had a crush on her forever. We met way back in the first grade and have been friends ever since." Jimmy closed his eyes and appeared to drift off, maybe reminiscing about moments in the past or dreaming of wonderment yet to come. "I always tried to push for more," he sighed. "She hasn't given in yet; says she's worried about losing the family she has now—losing what we have as 'friends' over some short-lived fling. I've always told myself, 'Someday, you're going to show Sue Ellen you're the one for her. You're the one for her...and she's the one for you!'" I could feel Jimmy straining to share just a bit of his long-ago-buried bliss with me.

Sometimes I really hate my job. I act on someone else's arbitrary decisions—someone I don't know and will probably never meet. The contracts are filtered down to me for execution, sometimes relayed through a contact I trust, or maybe in a note secured for my eyes only. I have no knowledge of the circumstances leading to my orders, nor do I know what the aftermath will be—except that the decision will end a life and ruin countless others.

I used to wonder why my boss never dealt with me in person. Meeting face-to-face would help me get a better feel for the impact of my work, and it would give them the opportunity to relish in the masterpieces I create for them.

Now I know why. They don't want any part of what Jimmy and I do.

"She's your target."

I can't begin to imagine the mountain of emotions and questions pouring through Jimmy's mind. Maybe I didn't want to know because I didn't want to think about how I would react if I were in his shoes.

"Why?"

"Can't we pick someone else?"

"What if I can't do this?"

"Why?"

But, Jimmy showed none of those reactions, no emotion at all. His only tell was the change in his eyes. With a renewed lifeless stare, he asked one question only.

"By when?"

I gave him until noon the next day. He tracked down Sue Ellen Kapict early. Apparently, she loved quiet time in her garden and spent every Saturday morning, from eight to eleven o'clock, caring for her plants and flowers.

For our after-action review, I chose to go without details. All I needed to know was asked and answered in one question. "Was it gruesome?" Jimmy's eyes lit up once more as his smile spread from ear to ear.

"Oh, yeah," he cooed, "and I definitely sent a message."

Sue Ellen's death hit that quaint town hard, more so than the other recent murders. Of course, there was talk of a connection between the killings. Residents were afraid to walk the streets alone. Police had no leads. They couldn't even come up with a motive. Finally, the town rose up. It was if they all screamed in unison, "Enough!" To help fade the stain of yet another gruesome murder in Bakers, Todd Kapict organized Bakers Township Community Day, with a parade, a genuine county fair, and capped off by a sweetheart dance in the evening. The event was scheduled for the nineteenth, a mere three weeks after Sue Ellen was murdered. Three weeks was pretty quick considering everything Todd had to accomplish: bury his love, start a new life alone, and plan this event.

Twenty-one days was hardly enough time.

For Jimmy, twenty-one days was an eternity. He marveled at his accomplishments during the previous seven, eyes sparkling with the recollection of every blade strike...every inch of skin peeled from the bitch who had rejected him so many times. Now, as he prepared to celebrate his retribution, he worked side by side with Todd to ensure everything was just right. Todd was indebted to Jimmy for rounding up Sue Ellen's old friends and encouraging them to participate in the day's festivities.

"You were always good to her, Jimmy," Todd softly sobbed. "Thank you."

Jimmy smiled. "I just want to continue to be a big part of this."

The night before the festivities, I sat down with Jimmy and asked him, "Are you ready for this?"

"Ready for what?" Jimmy squared his jaw, taking a deep breath of the stale country air. "Community Day? I fucking love it. I'm going to enjoy watching these people fake happiness through their bloodshot eyes, welled up with tears." He struck a mock pose of monumental sorrow hiding under a whisper-thin veil of cheer. I figured that was going to be his look for Community Day.

Everything was set up perfectly for the plan, if I do say so myself. The time had come to rattle Jimmy's cage. Payback for being such an asshole, for being so good at this job. "Tomorrow's the date."

With his head cocked to the side, like that RCA dog staring at the phonograph, he asked, "Date for what?"

"Kill number five. In a public place. The dance." The kid was cold. He had no reaction, no flinch of surprise or look of concern.

Again, he had just one question. "Who's the target?"

My instructions were simple. I told him, "Your pick, Jimmy. The only requirement is it's gotta be at the sweetheart dance. Everything else is up to you. Just brief me on the details when the job is done." The corner of Jimmy's mouth turned up into a smirk as his eyes closed softly. Slowly rocking his head, he seemed to be in full agreement with the plan he was unfolding. I could tell the kid already had his pigeon in mind.

The need to justify my existence, to at least pretend I was teaching my pupil something, forced me to keep talking. "You'll need a woman, you know. Can't really go to a sweetheart dance on your own now, can you?"

"I already got one." Of course he did. "Might as well go with the obvious choice," he affirmed.

"She doesn't know anything about your training, right?" I just couldn't stop talking.

"She's dumb as a box of rocks. That's probably why her first husband left her a few years back."

Jimmy and I parted, set to meet a week after the kill. If all went according to plan, Bakers Township would be a hornet's nest of activity. It was not exactly a good place or time to be a stranger walking around town, especially one with so many accomplishments under his belt. No matter how perfectly you covered your tracks, after so many jobs, inevitably a pattern would begin to emerge—they'd find that one piece and everything would fall into place. I needed to be long gone before someone had a chance to find mine. I left town immediately. Jimmy would disappear at some point after the hit.

I figured if Jimmy met me today, his plan had worked out. He disappeared, just another victim of the Bakers Township's killer, never to be seen again—as he started a storied career with the foundation. If it hadn't gone well, I'd move on. There's always another trainee waiting in the wings.

But, all went well.

From my booth in Diorgio's Coffee Shop, I had a clear view of the parking lot as well as the street feeding customers in. It was the perfect place to meet. Diorgio's has the best bagels and lox in this part of the country. Plus, it's a little over two hundred miles away from Bakers Township, well outside of the search area they had set up.

If it weren't for that dopey walk of his, I wouldn't have even recognized Jimmy when he turned the corner and shot a straight line for the door. He was empty-handed and dressed for a casual Saturday afternoon in town. A curly mop top, dark with just a hint of tangerine, covered up his blond buzz cut. The winter had been unseasonably cold, yet Jimmy's bronzed tan gave the impression that he lived in or had just returned from the islands. I just looked the same as before.

Jimmy asked the waitress for a cup of coffee—black, no sugar—as he slid into the booth across from me. "So, what's it now?" I asked. "James? Jim?" I offered alternatives in a playful tone. "Peter?

Antonio?" His only response was that lopsided smirk. Our waitress served him his coffee; he wrapped his hands around the mug.

"Fuck, it's cold out," was his opener. "I think I'll stick with Jimmy."

Gently tapping my near-empty cup, I whispered an announcement to the coffee shop's patrons, "Well, here's to the coronation of Jimmy the Kid!" Jimmy blushed, sheepishly lowering his eyes to the table. That humble gesture was one of the rare times I saw anything other than the devil himself in the kid. Satan returned, however, the instant I started his debrief.

"Walk me through it."

Jimmy looked straight through me. With no inflection in his voice, no emotion, he detailed Community Day. "I chose Todd Kapict because he was definitely the highest-profile target at the time. I figured no better way to send the message than by striking at the heart of our fair community. Besides, he had nothing left. I honestly felt sorry for the poor bastard, probably did him a favor."

"You're a saint," I joked. *You're the devil made flesh,* I thought. But Jimmy was in a trance. My sarcasm was lost on him. He needed to tell his story, to relive his glory.

"With Gina as my puppet, we were the perfect combination. Blending in like we did, no one thought we were there for any reason other than to celebrate Community Day. We also stuck out just enough, with Gina's knockout body and her sad story. She acted like she was crazy about me. Everyone will remember our genuine love for each other. One of us actually believing that ruse made it look so much better."

Jimmy described how he worked the room, solidifying his fictional account and clouding the timeline so his momentary absence during the dance went unnoticed. Later, when the police interviewed witnesses, Christine remembered that she talked to Jimmy and he had told her about how sad Mike was. Mike had talked about Jimmy consoling Christine right after he had been joking with Bobby. Bobby remembered...

Witness statements, especially concerning violent crimes, tend to have a lot of holes. He was just a kid. It took me years to develop a knack for pre-staging a crime scene like that. Jimmy was already putting me to shame.

He told me how Todd was in a world of his own, attending to every little detail and ensuring the guests were having a great time.

Did they like the food? Did they need more to drink? What song did they want to hear next?

"I followed Todd," Jimmy continued, "out the back of the building. He was hauling another one of those big trash bags. You know, the one where you stick four or five garbage-can-sized bags into one? Anyway, we got to talking about Sue Ellen. I opened up about the love I'd felt for her all these years. I talked about my desire to be with her, to give everything to her and take all that she had. The poor sap, he didn't even get offended by my talk of carnal desire for his girl. He just felt my pain."

Jimmy's eyes lit up again.

"Todd leaned in to console me. That's when I struck!" he said, wrapping his left arm around an imaginary neck while he thrust his right fist up through an imaginary middle. "I used my trusty pick again, right to the back of his skull. Instant. No mess. I still wanted gruesome, although I had to be careful not to get anything on me. Going back to the dance with Todd's blood all over my suit would not be a smart move now, would it?"

"No," I confirmed, "it would not."

"So, anyway, I'm guessing you saw the pictures."

"I did, Jimmy. Great job. They're disgusting," I said, full of praise. *You're disgusting,* I thought, detesting him.

"Thanks," he beamed, deaf to my inner words, though I'm sure he would savor my disgust so much more than any praise I could offer.

"So, you made it back to Gina, no problem?"

"Well...I did get caught going back in."

"What?" Jimmy's confession caught me off guard for sure. "What the hell happened?"

"I was back in the building, walking down the hallway, when that old jackass, Mr. Stynes, ran into me."

Before I could ask him more questions, he started to laugh uncontrollably.

"He's the facilities manager...the janitor! He was just picking up the few remnants Todd overlooked when he was cleaning. Anyway, Stynes wanted to know what I was doing away from the party."

"'I was just going to the bathroom, Mr. Stynes,' I told him. I was fully prepared to use my ice pick again."

"Did you have to?" I tried to recall reading anything about a second killing.

“No,” Jimmy snorted in between a full-blown case of the giggles. “He just said, ‘Well, you just get back in the auditorium. I know your mother, and she would not be happy to find you roaming the hallways. Now, get!’” Jimmy could barely finish a sentence, let alone string two of them together. He was finding comedic undertones everywhere. “I was laughing so hard when I went back in, Mom kept asking me, ‘What’s so funny? What’s so funny?’ I just told her I was dead tired and wanted to go home. I was almost in control of myself by the time we left the building.” He paused, raising one finger before finishing his thought. “Then, I looked at the banner Todd had me paint.” The kid could barely gasp enough air. “You remember the one, right?” The nonsensical images had taken complete control of Jimmy.

“Yeah, I remember the banner.”

BAKERS TOWNSHIP MIDDLE SCHOOL
Parent-Student Sweetheart Dance
Open your heart to your kids and they will open theirs for you

Jimmy damn near fell out of the booth as he pounded his hand flat on the table again and again. “Get it?”

I got it, Jimmy.

He leaned in close to let me in on the punch line, figuring grown-ups just don't get the real funny stuff. "Get it? He opened his heart to Sue Ellen!"

I got it, Jimmy.

"Just like she did!"

He was just a kid.

His Story, His Way

It was a Tuesday.

Nobody knew who the hell Spencer Tucker was when he walked up to the administration desk of the Red Falls, Virginia Police Department and laid his palms directly on the plexiglass divider, staining the window with fog and spit from each excited breath. Tanya was not amused by the fat man in a velour jogging suit.

"Sir, can you please take your hands off the glass!" she insisted. It was not a question.

Spencer complied, though he continued his fight for air. Sweat dripped from handprints left behind on the glass. It disgusted Tanya.

"Can I help you with something?" Fatty was hunched over now, hands on his knees as he continued to snort and wheeze. Tanya didn't get paid enough for this shit, so she picked up the desk phone to call an officer down from the briefing room, but stopped when she saw the guy had one finger raised in the air.

She could see beads of sweat dripping down his digit and gagged at the thought of the god-awful mess underneath his mass.

Spencer had nearly caught his breath. With his finger still raised, he stood straight and inhaled a few more mouthfuls of air before he could speak. Once he started, he wouldn't shut up.

"Sorry about that," he blurted.

"I just started running again," he confessed.

"I'm trying to get back in shape," he proclaimed.

"You know, there was a time I could run five miles without breaking a sweat," he boasted.

The sentences grew longer as his need to suck in so much oxygen tapered off.

Tanya peeked over the counter to get a better look at the guy. He could see the disdain in her eyes, the judgment she was sending his way from behind her square hipster glasses, her overblown bleached-blond hair, and a liberal application of makeup, all brutalizing every modern fashion trend out there. "Sir, is there something I can help you with?" Spencer noticed a little more twang in her slight Southern accent this time.

"Yes, there is." Spencer was now quite composed. "I would like to report a murder." *That ought to get her attention.* The thought made him smirk. But for the excess blush on her cheekbones, all color faded from Tanya's face. She pulled open the top drawer of her desk, grabbed a "Criminal Complaint" form, and checked the "Violent" box on the top left. She took a second to compose herself before looking up again.

Yes, it's me. The poor man who must be going through hell right now. Spencer was savoring his feeling of control.

"You want to report a murder," she echoed while completing the form.

"Three murders, actually."

"Three?"

"Did I say three?" Spencer reared his head back and belted out a jolly laugh, as if Santa Claus himself had stopped by the police station to report a homicide. "I meant to say four. Four murders."

Tanya stopped writing and looked back up.

"So, it's four murders?"

"Yes." Spencer could clearly see the form she was writing on. He could also see that all she had written was "Murde" in the

"Complaint Description" section. *I never even got a full word out of her.*

"Do you know who committed these murders?" She posed the question in that singsong intonation you use when speaking to a child. *Annoying, but that's okay,* he figured. *This is probably the first time she's had to document such a heinous act, let alone four of them.*

"I do...umm...what's your name?"

"Tanya," she said, looking down at her desk, slowly tapping her pen against the nameplate–TANYA was written across its front.

"Tanya," Spencer chuckled. "Yeah, I can see that now, right there. Tanya, I committed the murders. All four killings."

She didn't write another thing, leaving that one almost-word her only entry on the form. *Surely, even if no one believes me, even if they think my statement–my confession–is a farce, they have to take my complaint and document it. Maybe she's waiting to get more information? Maybe she wants to see if my story and details are going to change again.* That one word stuck in his head: details.

"Oh, I see," he declared, realizing his mistake with the confession. "When I say I committed the murders, I didn't actually do the killing. I orchestrated the whole thing. Masterminded, if you will. I have people who do my dirty work." Spencer stood a bit taller after his proclamation.

Tanya dropped her pen to the desk, pointed at a single metal chair that definitely wouldn't accommodate his mass, and instructed, "Okay. Umm, why don't you go ahead and take a seat right over there. I'm just going to make a quick call and have some of my people come out here. Maybe they can get together with your people and we can figure out what happened here. Okay, hun?" She picked up the phone and made a call.

Spencer had no intention of trying to sit in the chair, not for her simple amusement. He stood close to the window, hoping to overhear the conversation, but Tanya had turned her back to him. Spencer Tucker tapped on the pane repeatedly until she gave in and turned back around.

"Five, Tanya. I'm sorry. The actual number is five."

Sensing that Tanya had had enough, Spencer turned from the window and walked into the waiting area. First, he pulled out his phone and fired off a few text messages, none of which received a reply. Then, he began to gauge what exactly he was up against. *It doesn't seem like there's going to be much of an intellectual battle here, not if this is the best they have.* Sizing up the competition—that's how he liked to describe it—Spencer rummaged through the notes and flyers tacked on the bulletin board. Barbecues, community workshops, lost dogs, found dogs—to him, they all seemed to blend into one never-ending, pointless theme: life here is dull. One of the faded-wallpapered walls was adorned with eight by ten glossies in cheesy frames, hanging on nails randomly scattered across its surface. Three retirement ceremonies, two volunteer-of-the-month awards, and a recent graduating class of the Teen Citizen's Police Academy highlighted everything he needed to know about Red Falls. *For a town not even one hundred miles outside of DC, everything turns real rural here, real quick.*

After twenty minutes, Spencer's critique of the station's decor was interrupted when three police officers entered the reception area and approached him. No guns were drawn, but hands were hovering close. The officer in the middle broke the silence. "Sir, do you have any weapons on your person right now?" Spencer shook his head defiantly, sending his jowl and chins into rippling convulsions.

"Nope. Personally, I'm scared to touch them."

"Are you in any danger right now?"

"I don't think so. Am I?"

"Do you know of anyone else in danger right now?" The question made Spencer pause, as if he didn't know which answer would be more entertaining. With a slight grin, he decided to go with, "No. Final answer."

He was instructed to follow the officers, two leading, one following, into the back so they could take his statement. Once inside, Spencer looked around. *Not impressive. How can they conduct an official interrogation from a round table? And, the room is carpeted! I don't think the good crime dramas have carpeted interrogation rooms. Either way, it's not safe. It's not even sanitary.* With a little kitchenette in the corner housing a sink, fridge, and microwave, Spencer realized he was in their break room.

He was invited to sit at the round table while the officers stood over him. *Is this supposed to be intimidating? The only interrogating that is going to happen here is, "Who stole my leftover hoagie?" What a joke!* The lead officer introduced himself and the other two, then explained the objectives of the interview. The officers muddled their way through a script like TV reporters trying to fill five minutes of dead air after finishing the last news story. Spencer drifted in and out. *This is all so disappointing. And they haven't even asked my name yet.*

"And you, sir. Can you give me your full name, please?"

"Huh?" Spencer asked. Sergeant Daniels had caught him by surprise. Daniels knew that was going to happen. He could tell by the eyes. Whenever someone came into a police station—no matter if they were a criminal, complainant, or witness—and everything started to overwhelm them, they got that look. Daniels loved to snap them back by turning the conversation over to them. "Your name, sir. Can I please get your full name?"

"Oh. Sure. Tucker. Spencer Tucker." Spencer thought for a moment, then clarified. "No middle initial. Just Spencer Tucker." Daniels acknowledged this with a nod before moving on to date of birth, home address, employment status, marital status...

"Marital status?" A bit of a smirk, the check-this-shit-out kind, spread across Spencer's face as he looked at the officer on his left, Bridle, then on his right, Donnelly. *Check this shit out!* "That's a tricky one, Sergeant Daniels. My wife, Vicki, is one of my victims."

Daniels could feel the hair on the back of his neck stiffen and stand. This was his alert, his warning signal. If nineteen years on the force had taught him anything, it was that when something raised the hair on the back of his neck, there was fixing to be trouble. He opened his notepad, scribbled a few lines, pulled the sheet off, and handed it to Officer Donnelly.

Spencer Tucker

Pull anything you can

Find his wife. Vicki

Without a word, Donnelly was off. "Bridle," said Sergeant Daniels, "can you check and see if Interview Room A is available?"

"Sure thing, Sarge." Spencer and Daniels were alone.

Spencer Tucker was no longer a fat buffoon lost in a fantasy world. Spencer Tucker had just put a name to his victim. Neither man spoke another word until Bridle returned, confirming the room was open. Finally, Spencer Tucker was going to get the treatment he felt he was due. Officer Bridle patted him down, kneading his sweaty jogging suit pants to confirm there were no weapons; he was only carrying a wallet and phone. Both were bagged for safekeeping.

Spencer was escorted down the hall and into Interview Room A. Looking around, he smiled. *Now, this is more like it! Barren walls. A rectangular table. No rug. But where's the video camera? Do they mount it at the end of the table or use a standing tripod? They don't have a two-way mirror—how disappointing. But this is a significant improvement.*

Daniels read Spencer Tucker his Miranda rights and asked if he wanted a lawyer present. Spencer declined. "No lawyer. I have a better idea."

"What do you propose, Mr. Tucker?"

"Simple. I'll tell you everything you need to know. I just want to be able to tell my story, my way."

"That's it?" Daniels kept his part of the conversation short; letting a perp talk was usually the best starting approach. If they felt like they were in charge, they usually started singing. That made getting to the truth much easier. Daniels figured that if this guy turned out to be a crackpot, his own words would be his one-way ticket to the psych ward. If he was guilty, and the reality of his crime felt like too much of a burden for him, a confession would be his redemption—and his conviction.

"That's it, Sergeant Daniels." Spencer looked around, like a lion overseeing his domain as he decides where to strike first. "Now this is an interrogation room," he mused. "Where's the video recorder?"

Daniels held up his cell phone. "We don't usually shoot video, Mr. Tucker. We just record the interview from our phones here." He could tell Spencer wasn't satisfied with the answer. "Would you like us to use a video recorder, Mr. Tucker?"

"I think the brutality of my crimes warrants a filmed confession, don't you?" The sergeant nodded at Bridle, who stood up, left the room, and promptly returned with a video camera. No one spoke for the next few minutes while the camera was being set up. Spencer was wondering just how far he could push this, gauging how much control he possessed. Daniels was wondering the same, though he was calculating how much rope to give Tucker.

The camera was placed at one end of the table, on top of an empty cardboard box, since Bridle couldn't find the tripod. Spencer sat at the other end of the table, his arms spread leisurely across its otherwise empty surface. When the red light turned on, and Bridle confirmed, "We're running," the stage was Spencer's.

"Can I get something to drink? A pop, maybe?" This was not the opening statement Daniels was expecting.

"Mr. Tucker, you are trying my patience here. If a crime was committed, let's get on with it. If not, this charade is about to rack you up a whole slew of charges. Now, why don't we—"

"Vicki Tucker," Spencer cut the sergeant off. Suddenly, jolly transformed to evil, a mood change that caught fire in an instant, flushing his fat face from pasty white to blazing red. "My wife, Vicki Tucker. She was my fourth victim."

Showing no emotion, Daniels continued writing notes on his pad. "Who were the first three?"

"Where's my pop?" Another nod from the sergeant sent Bridle off again. "The regular kind," Spencer yelled after the young officer. "That diet stuff is no good for you."

Spencer got his pop, the regular kind. His face had returned to what was probably its normal color. He was ready to talk. "I met Vicki at a Christmas party almost six years ago," he began. "She was drop-dead gorgeous. She had it all. I mean, she had the long blond hair, nice firm tits. Not like those ridiculously over-pumped silicone ones. No, hers were nice. And her body was tight. I mean, she could've had her own Pornhub channel, it was that nice. And she kept it nice."

Bridle squirmed in his chair a bit, kind of hoping Donnelly would find some photographs of Spencer's wife. Sergeant Daniels took a different course. "So, you two hit it off, I guess?" Bridle snickered a bit, imagining a gorgeous body like hers pinned under Spencer Tucker. One look from his boss, however, and he clammed up. If there was one thing Daniels hated in this world, it was having to care for these damn rookie cops. Wipe their nose. Tell them when to speak, when not to speak, and when not to giggle like a six-year-old schoolgirl.

"I'm not an idiot, gentlemen. I know how fat I am. I weighed 347 pounds this morning. Although that is three pounds less than last week."

Daniels just wanted to get him back on topic and to keep him talking. "Officer Bridle has a little difficulty controlling himself." Daniels shot Bridle another look that clearly meant, *Keep your fucking mouth shut.* "Self-control is clearly a trait that comes with age. Mr. Tucker, please go on."

"Anyway," he continued, staring straight into the camera, "I was a lot slimmer six years ago. Not skinny, just thinner. I think I was about two-fifty-ish when Vicki and I met, but I had something that won her desire one thousand times over. I had lots and lots of money!"

Daniels wrote a note on his pad: "MONEY," accenting his speculation with two firm underlines.

"I made my millions as a defense contractor, writing software applications for the military. Our Christmas party that first year served a dual purpose: commemorating the birth of our Lord and Savior, Jesus Christ, and the successful test of my satellite targeting algorithm. We could shoot a laser from space, vaporizing a single terrorist standing in a schoolyard full of children without any collateral damage."

Spencer Tucker leaned back and closed his eyes. He could smell the seared flesh, the result of his computer code. *But, this is not the time to reminisce about past exploits. We're here to discuss your most recent achievement.* "Anyway," he summarized, "blah, blah, blah. The sex was incredible for me. We got married six months later and moved out here about five years ago."

Daniels seized the opportunity to poke his first hole. "Well, I've been in Red Falls all my life, been a cop here for more years than I care to remember. I never heard of a multimillionaire defense contractor living here in town."

"Exactly," Spencer shut the question down. "We live outside of the city boundary. Well, we lived...or is it *she* lived?" With a quick smirk and a shrug of his shoulders, he moved on. "No matter. It's unincorporated no-man's land, I guess. I don't get out much, usually just stay home writing code and getting fatter, but Vicki took a lot of trips to DC with her friend, Samantha." Spencer felt it was time. "She was number three." Daniels and Bridle both snapped their heads up, Daniels from his fourth page of notes, Bridle from his lethargy.

"Samantha was the third victim?" That question came from Daniels. Bridle knew better than to talk.

With his attention directed to the sergeant, Spencer Tucker replied, "She was. Samantha Eppling. And her prick fuck husband, Robbie, was the second." *Now, we finally get to square off, Sergeant.* For the first time, a new shade of crimson brushed across Spencer's face.

"And who was the first?"

"Jeremy Poshure."

"Why him?"

"He fucked my wife."

Daniels knew his plan had worked. He'd let Tucker slip deeper and deeper into his own self-absorbed monologue until he could no longer control himself, sending the conversation exactly where the sergeant desired. All Daniels needed to do now was extract the details.

Spencer loved details. As a man who built his fortune using the most complex syntax in the world, he appreciated the importance of having every command, every subtask, properly formatted. If his plan compiled correctly, the result was a work of art. Spencer was exceptionally proud of his most celebrated compilation. *Now, all I need to do is share every detail with them.* He launched into it. "Vicki and Samantha enjoyed their DC excursions. They loved to shop and gossip.

"The problem was that Samantha truly loved her husband, Robbie. Their marriage was a goddamn fairy tale." Spencer's face showed disgust, not jealousy, as he described their magic. "Two gorgeous people madly in love with each other, both driven to succeed, both independently rich. Then, there was my wife, Vicki. She was dumber than shit and, without question, had no interest in earning her prosperity. She found sex with me repugnant but stuck around because I had the wealth she craved. But, you know, we were a happy couple, just living separate lives that occasionally crossed to satisfy my lust for sex and Vicki's desire for affluence."

Spencer went on to describe the strain in their marriage. As he did, Sergeant Daniels learned how Spencer's insecurities about keeping a woman of Vicki's caliber led him to hire a private investigator. The PI's audio and video recordings of conversations between his wife and Samantha ended up substantiating Spencer's fears. He said that Vicki craved love. She longed for passion, when it was the result of being the object of attraction as well as when she felt that uncontrollable desire for someone else. As far as he could tell, Samantha and Robbie Eppling kept no secrets from each other. The PI told Spencer they were the ones who hatched the plan to introduce Vicki to a guy named Jeremy Poshure.

"When my contact first showed me pictures of Vicki and Jeremy together, I was devastated. I found out they slept together less than three hours after they met."

Spencer's grim attitude softened for a moment. "I planned to confront her, but when she got home that day, she acted so happy. It had been a while since I'd seen her truly happy. When she was happy, she made me very happy." Bridle contained himself when images of a blond goddess making her fat guy "happy" popped into his head.

"So, I let it go for a while. I had my contact keep track of Jeremy and Vicki. It turns out Jeremy and Robbie were attorneys at the same law firm. Vicki and Samantha's trips to DC became more frequent. My wife started going to DC for the weekend by herself, though she always said she was with Samantha. It wasn't long before she was just driving to his house in Gates Ridge."

Spencer's eyes dropped and his arms slumped into his lap helplessly. For the first time, he looked defeated. "She still came home happy, but no longer shared her euphoria with me. I tried to rekindle the romance we feigned for many years by suggesting a month-long getaway in Hawaii. Do you know what she said?"

Spencer asked no one in particular. "She just pointed at me and said, 'I'm not going any place where you're allowed to walk around with those titties hanging out, but I can't.'

"When she returned from her fictitious DC trip that week, we had our last conversation. She was wearing this banana-cream sleeveless maxi dress. You know the kind? It hugs a woman's body all the way to the knees before flaring out?"

"Sure," was all Daniels could say as he watched Spencer's demeanor morph yet again.

"Well, she was wearing that with a matching floppy fedora. God, did she look amazing! As I looked at her–feeling her captivating radiance–the only thing I could say was, 'You are going to suffer for this.' That was the last time I ever spoke a word to my wife."

Daniels stared into the face of pure evil. For the first time in his career, he was scared to ask the next question. "So, what did you do next?"

"I talked," snickered the once-again jovial dumpling. He pushed the chair back to make room for his belly, kicked his feet out, and sunk down a bit before taking another sip of his beverage.

"I talked, and I talked, and I talked. Much like we're doing now, you see, but I wasn't conversing *with* her. I wasn't even talking *at* her or *to* her. Instead, I talked *around* her. Much like we're doing with your protégé here," pointing at Bridle, who was still sulking in his chair against the far wall, separated from the big boys' table. "Mostly, she just listened. Sometimes she would ask questions. Other times, she would beg and plead. But mostly, she sat there in horror as I detailed what I was going to do to Jeremy Poshure...then Robbie Eppling...then Samantha Eppling...and finally, to Vicki Tucker."

Sergeant Daniels kept his mouth shut as he weighed his options. The obvious choice was to stop the interview and call the medical staff over at County. He had never seen this level of detail in a delusional suspect before. Then again, what if the story was true? Was Tucker boasting of his sadistic accomplishments? Or did he feel remorse for his crimes?

Daniels realized Tucker had stopped talking. He was sitting quietly, waiting, with an ever-so-slight smirk on the left corner of his mouth. Daniels knew the guy was just waiting for him to continue to play the game, to indulge him. If the police wouldn't play their part, neither would he. Daniels cursed Donnelly for taking so long. "All right, Mr. Tucker," he said, giving in. "What exactly did you tell your wife?"

Officer Bridle leaned in closer, hungry for an answer, yet reluctant to imagine the horror he was about to hear. Spencer could see suspense building in the junior officer. *I bet you've never heard a tale like this before, skippy.* Bridle just stared into his eyes, unable to move, unwilling to talk. Spencer loved it. *I am going to give you nightmares for years...*

With a wave of his hand, Spencer continued. "Jeremy Poshure moved in fast on Vicki. It wasn't his fault. He was young and horny. I mean, he just wanted to get his dick wet. Then, they go and plop Vicki in front of him. Hell, I probably would've done the same thing he did. I didn't know Poshure and he didn't know me." With a vengeful gaze, he stared right through Daniels. "But then he got close with my wife. He pulled her in as she was pushing me out. So, he had just entered his apartment when they got him. One shot to the head. POW!" Tucker's hand slammed onto the table, the burst reverberating off the bare walls, sending the camera and its cardboard stand skipping across the table. (The rest of the interview was filmed at an unusual angle with the star slightly off-center, a mishap that Spencer thought ruined an otherwise flawless confession.)

"No, there was no need for him to endure pain." Daniels was sure there was more to the story. Tucker was too meticulous with the details of the rest of his fantasy. And there was.

"When Vicki first heard what I was going to do to these guys, I'm convinced she never imagined any of it would become reality." Spencer smiled the biggest smile his face could form, sat upright, and arched his back, as if he intended to dazzle the audience with his first presentation. "My, how everything changed when she opened the box with Jeremy's severed penis and a note card that said, 'So you will never be separated from your true love again.'"

Bridle and Daniels both squirmed uncomfortably, a sight Spencer cherished. Then, giggling in anticipation of the next scene, he moved on.

"Now, I'm sure you can imagine Vicki's reaction," he said matter-of-factly, "or maybe you can't. I'll admit, I had a hard time envisioning it myself, which is why I got a photographer. The shots are quite lovely. I'll have them sent to you when we're all done, okay?"

"Thank you, I guess." Daniels kept playing his part.

"You're quite welcome." Spencer kept going. "Anyway, after the Jeremy episode, I was sure Vicki would remember the pecking order I had described to her: Jeremy, Robbie, Samantha, and then, finally, her. I hoped she would run to her fellow conspirator, which she did, for the pictures I have of those two girls together when the second box was discovered are priceless." He sustained an ear-to-ear smile, making it clear that he was especially proud of the second murder.

Playing his role, Daniels asked, "You cut off Robbie's penis as well?"

"Oh, no, Sergeant. Robert Eppling was much more complicit in my betrayal. He violated my trust as a friend. He helped put this whole affair in motion. He was so much more than just a dick, so I took more. I carved out enough so the ladies knew exactly what I thought of that asshole prick."

Bridle silently prayed for the story to end. He knew there were still two to go, but he just needed Tucker to stop talking.

"It's almost a shame Vicki knew how the rest of this part of the story went. She could not bring herself to watch the videotape of my trophy being pulled while Robbie still took breath."

"Jesus!"

"Officer Bridle, do you need to go outside and take a moment?"

"No, Sergeant. I'm fine."

Daniels was hoping for a yes, unsure of how much more Bridle could stomach—or he himself, for that matter.

Oh, I can't have you give up just yet. Maybe I will extend you the slightest bit of compassion. After all, you did get me my pop! "I see my narrative is taking a toll on you both." No one responded. "Why don't I give you the rest in a condensed version?"

"You just go ahead and say what you feel you need to say, Mr. Tucker."

"Thank you, Sergeant Daniels." His momentary air of civility did not mask Tucker's thirst to relay the gruesome images with pride.

"Vicki ran, for fear of her life. Let's just say Ms. Samantha, the freshly crowned widow, expended way too much energy mourning the loss of her fortune. She watched helplessly as everything in her home was dismantled and destroyed. I took her passion. I took her possessions. With her hands bound together, holding a pistol to her face, I gave her the option: take her own life or watch me peel it from her bones. She chose the former."

Sergeant Daniels was ready to put an end to Tucker's games. Before he moved, there was a quick rap on the door. Officer Donnelly stuck his head into the room. "Hey, Sarge? Can I run some stuff by you?"

"One moment, Mr. Tucker." Daniels got up and rushed toward the hallway.

"Take your time, Sergeant Daniels. Me and Officer Bridle here will get ourselves acquainted."

Daniels looked over to the rookie. "Don't you say a fucking word."

"Yes, Sergeant." Bridle was glad Daniels had said that out loud. All he had to do was sit and stare at the wall while Tucker stared back at him, smiling.

Out in the hall, Donnelly beamed with pride. "It's all bullshit, Sarge. Whatever he's telling you is all bullshit. His wife is alive.

She's sitting right out in the waiting room. Apparently just came back from a trip to DC with a friend." Donnelly flipped through his notes.

"Samantha?"

"Yeah, that's it, Sarge. Samantha Eppling. But Mrs. Tucker says she doesn't understand any of it, says she and her husband haven't even had an argument."

After instructing Donnelly to go stay with Tucker's wife, Daniels stood still. For the briefest of moments, he considered the two debating cartoon images on his shoulders. The angel, who told him to follow procedure, stop the interview, and call in the County doctors. Obviously, Tucker was crazy. The devil was agitated by the wasted afternoon and having to sit there listening to the deranged stories, stories that would probably give Bridle nightmares for a month. He decided it was his turn to play games.

He returned to Interview Room A, casually took his seat, and looked over to Officer Bridle. "Where were we?"

"Um, we had just finished hearing about the incident with Samantha Eppling, Sergeant."

"That's right. Samantha Eppling." He turned to Spencer. "Mr. Tucker, I believe you were going to talk about your wife now? Vicki Tucker?" Spencer detected Daniels' sudden air of superiority. He fought off the urge to make the sergeant his nemesis, as there was still one last story to tell.

"It's obvious you've grown bored with me, Sergeant. To be honest, I am also fatigued. But I will tell you, Vicki got exactly what she wanted. Once she came out of hiding–you know she couldn't hide forever–I had her taken to a special location. There, she spent the rest of her life in a room not much bigger than this." He scanned over all six sides of Interview Room A, nodding in agreement. "Yep. Not much bigger than this room at all. She was surrounded by everything she wanted. Lots of money. Lots of jewelry. And her friends Jeremy, Robbie, and Samantha. Well, at least what remained of them."

"So, she just stayed there?" Sergeant Daniels tried to imagine how a person could create such a fantasy.

"Of course not. What kind of loving husband would I be if I didn't leave a gift of my own?"

"Not much of one," Daniels mocked.

"No," he agreed, "not much at all. On the walls, I arranged photographs of her three friends in all their glory. Two televisions, mounted high out of her reach, blared videos: the final moments of Robbie and Samantha Eppling. It's amazing how long a body can last before surrendering to famine, thirst, and insanity. Yes, indeed, Vicki Tucker died with everything she wanted."

"And what about victim five? You mentioned there were five victims."

"Yes, that's right. Of no significance," Spencer said, waving his hand as if sweeping the air clean. "I don't even know the poor fool's whole name."

The sergeant beamed as he stood up. "My turn." Picking up his phone, he called the contact already pulled. "Yeah, bring the witness in now." Daniels turned to Spencer Tucker with a smile, placing a hand on his shoulder.

"Mr. Tucker, your story is indeed a fantastic tale. I'd like to bring in someone who, I think you'll agree, has a slightly better version." He walked over and opened the door. Officer Bridle nearly fell out of his chair when he saw Vicki Tucker standing in the doorway very much alive. She was as beautiful as Spencer had described.

Spencer Tucker looked over at his wife and hissed, “You are going to suffer for this.” Vicki jerked back in surprise, dropping her banana-cream fedora.

Spencer Tucker had been in County Psychiatric for ten days when Vicki found a package on her doorstep.

No one has seen Tanya for a week.

...in abeyance

I - Friday, March 28, 2014

PORTLAND, OREGON

Almost Midnight

It's standard fare in a hospital's emergency room—fiery, passionate scenes play out between the most peculiar of couples, suddenly bonded close though they met just minutes before. These scenes often pass unnoticed. For some, however, such bonds change everything.

Christopher Baxter, MD, portrayed the image of a doctor in control. Even in the most desperate situations, he remained poised and focused on what he needed to do to save lives. His reputation for being so calm and collected was the reason Dr. Baxter's outburst startled his ER team so.

"Come on, you son of a bitch!" Chris pleaded as he continued beating into the lifeless body below with his bare fist.

Three pale-white walls monotonously outlined the room not quite large enough to agreeably hold its four occupants, further interrupted by random carts full of medical supplies. The fourth wall, an impersonal vinyl "modesty" curtain, was thrown back in a harried effort to make way for additional supplies or equipment. Chris's irritation with the helpless form increased; for the two nurses, the pale-white walls, so calming earlier in the day, seemed to darken and close in tighter. Both were too startled by his behavior to interrupt. Instead, they focused on the job at hand, anxiously following procedure and the direction of the on-call doctor.

Chris hated when they flatlined on his watch. Even in a room where death was so commonplace, he felt contempt when someone's heart just stopped. To him, it was such an uncivilized finale, souring everything that makes up who a person was, the dreams they probably had, and the life they probably led. When a patient like this came in—a man of similar athletic build, appearing quite a bit younger than Chris—heart failure hit home harder than other, more age-appropriate causes of death, even here in this insensitive room. Chris sighed, "It's going to be one of those weekends."

Early is on time, on time is late.

John Doe was Chris's first patient to walk through the doors that night. Twenty minutes before his thirty-six-hour shift officially started, this man, this random face, walked in through the main door of the emergency room and collapsed. No request for help or other warning preceded his sudden drop. If he had walked through the doors, strolled the entire waiting area, and left, most likely no one would have even noticed him. Instead, his collapse kicked the staff into action on this otherwise quiet night. The man arrived alone, no family or friends. Not even a wallet to identify him.

The irony of the scene was not lost on Chris. To him, "early is on time, on time is late" was not just a catchphrase. The quip was a valuable lesson he learned years ago. It was US Army logic at its finest: hurry up and wait—wait and wait if you must, just don't be late. There was a reason this routine came to him so naturally. He believed in the logic, for it had proved itself true, time and again.

Early is on time, on time is late.

As Chris continued the seemingly futile efforts to save John Doe's life, his mind faded back a few months earlier to another patient—little Tommy McGrath. Tommy could so easily have ended up in the same grim situation as the unfortunate Mr. Doe, but that night, Chris was early. He had arrived on time to save a life.

* * *

Tommy's leg hurt. That underwhelming description was the best the eight-year-old boy was able to give his mother, and all she could relay to the doctor. Late on a Tuesday evening, after helplessly watching her child suffer for two days, Ellen decided her best option was to bring him to the hospital. Really, it was her only option, as any other meant another long, sleepless night for both of them, and they would probably end up going to the ER in the morning anyway.

* * *

Standing over John Doe, Chris scanned the room, searching for something to rescue him from his current dilemma. He gazed longingly at the crash cart, crowned with his long-time ally in the noble fight to preserve life, the PIC 50 defibrillator with its long, thin heart monitor leads adhered to his patient's chest–the lamprey searching inside a host for possible signs of life. Its charging paddles remained nestled in their cradle, worthless for the time being. Even though "Old Betty" was now considered a dinosaur, Chris refused to part ways with her. The model was a throwback to his army days, purchased by Saint Augustus on his insistence. Old Betty quickly lived up to her reputation; in nearly three years, she had saved the lives of 135 patients.

Chris's only offer to the paddles was one of solace. "You won't be needed today, my friends." After all these years, Baxter still found humor that there are just some things you'll never learn from television. Yelling "Clear!" and bringing a body back to life by simply pressing the paddles to a chest, is one of those lessons.

Of course, that isn't how it works. When a heart stops completely–when there are no electrical pulses surging through the body at all–a defibrillator is of no use. At this point, the only options are clearing the patient's airway, administering high-dose epinephrine, and slamming your clenched fist onto the patient's chest with a precordial thump. Unfortunately, these methods rarely work. The fact is, when they do flatline, even the most advanced attempts prove themselves unsuccessful.

* * *

"Where does it hurt, Tommy?" The doctor on call that night tried his best to ease the frightened boy. The timid physician wasn't willing to say his patient was fabricating his pain, but he just couldn't find anything wrong. He had already sent Tommy up to the fourth floor for x-rays and down to the second floor to for a full spectrum of blood tests. The boy was then brought back to the ER to wait some more. Each department double-checked their results. No test, no doctor, nothing could explain the boy's suffering. As far as they could determine, there was nothing to find.

For such a young boy, Tommy was unusually calm throughout the evening. His mother wasn't surprised by this; her son was used to the hospital, having been admitted countless times over his few years battling pediatric Crohn's disease. But this time, his cries of pain told his worried mom something was different. She explained to the doctor, "My boy knows about pain. He doesn't like it and wouldn't make something like this up."

"We're looking, Mrs. McGrath. We just don't see anything. Your son has been through quite a bit over the years. He may be remembering the discomfort from prior visits. That's not uncommon."

Crying wails of pain erupted from Tommy again. The doctor looked at the boy's mother and shyly winced in preparation for what was coming next.

"He's not faking it!"

* * *

Death had arrived. The small room continued to cramp. As the once-white scene took on a sickeningly opaque and gloomy light, both nurses checked and rechecked the leads to the monitor, hoping for a miracle. Nurse Sarah Levy moved methodically and efficiently. She stared down at the patient, searching for any signs of life—the slightest muscle twitch or movement under closed eyelids—then checked to see if the monitor had been able to find any activity. When there was nothing to note, she looked at Chris for further instructions. Without a response from him, she would continue following protocol. Something would eventually change, but what, when, and how, she didn't know. She looked out through the open curtain to see what kind of attention they were attracting (the gaggle of spectators—staff, patients, and visitors—had grown to about seven), then at Nurse Charger to share a destitute look of "What do we do next?"

Penny Charger was in her own state of limbo, her own repetitive loop of procedures slightly ahead of, or possibly slightly behind, her friend's. Neither of them spoke a word, but their expressions were the same: "I have no idea." Everything was on hold as this end-of-life crisis played out around them. Something would soon change, but not because of Rachel's or Penny's interference.

* * *

"He's not faking it!" Ellen McGrath insisted.

"No, not faking. It's a recall of past trauma, Mrs. McGrath. We are going to admit him for tonight. We can treat the pain he thinks is there. In the meantime, we'll run more tests, but there's not much we can do without an injury, infection, or anything else to treat."

The night staff was prepping Tommy McGrath for admission to the general ward that night when Chris came in, twenty minutes before his shift was scheduled to start.

Early is on time, on time is late.

The on-call doctor appeared to be dangerously close to tipping the scale of Ellen McGrath's emotions. It was evident that she was fighting to control her rage over the doctor's suggestion of "phantom pain," a term that should never be used to describe what a chronically ill patient is feeling, especially a child, and never in front of their family. Chris milled about the triage area, sizing up the cast of patients he would work with that night. He quickly took note of the exchange between the doctor and Mrs. McGrath. Nurse Charger filled him in on their situation.

It took Dr. Baxter about twenty seconds to know where this was going. He knew better than to insert himself into another doctor's conversation with a patient's mother, so he strolled over to chat with Tommy and to scan his chart.

- Complaint: pain, upper right leg
- X-ray: negative
- White blood cell count: normal
- Medical history: pediatric Crohn's disease

Chris broke the ice. "Tommy, is it?"

"Uh-huh." The boy had a grim expression.

"Yeah, I figured that. It says Thomas right here on the sheet, but you look like a Tommy. I had a buddy I went to medical school with–Thomas Andrew Radkinson-Forthnight Jr. Can you imagine that? Two people in the world named Thomas Andrew Radkinson-Forthnight, and the other one ends up being his father. So, to make it worse, he had to live with Thomas Andrew Radkinson-Forthnight Jr.!"

Distracting the boy, turning his attention from the pain, was Chris's goal. The smile that began to peek out of the corners of

Tommy's mouth was all Chris needed to see before continuing. In the most serious tone he could muster, Chris stood straight and tall. "Well, for Thomas Andrew Radkinson-Forthnight, to have to bear the insult of being called a junior would just not do. He insisted on being called Tommy."

Tommy leaned forward and uttered a gasp of wonderment as he listened to the story. "Really?"

"Yep. Tommy Rad! That's his name now. He had it legally changed when he grew up. Pretty cool, huh?"

"Wow! You can do that?"

"Yep. He went to court to change his name and everything. It's a done deal!"

"Is that for real?"

"One hundred percent absolutely positively for real. Hey, how'd you like to have me give him a call? You can have your prescriptions signed by Tommy Rad, MD."

Smiles widened on both of them.

"Doctor Rad!"

Tommy let out a full-blown giggle. While they were talking, Chris had been gently pressing on points up and down the sick boy's right leg. When he touched mid-thigh, Tommy let out the tiniest whimper, trying to be brave. He turned his head to wipe away a single tear, ashamed to look weak in front of his new friend.

In a subdued voice, Chris reassured him, "It's okay, Tommy. We'll figure this out." Snapping straight and tall again, Chris winked, then turned to talk to the attending nurse to ask about the boy's symptoms and review his medication history.

On the list: prednisone.

Chris had seen this reaction before. He quickly examined Tommy again. With this much pain, and no injury to attribute it to, or visible sign of irritation or inflammation, Chris suspected that Tommy was fighting an infection. In fact, he had probably been battling an infection even before the pain in his leg started. When he was being treated for Crohn's disease, Tommy was prescribed a cocktail of medications, each of which could have serious side effects. To aid these vile treatments, he was given prednisone as an immunosuppressant, as this could stop the body's natural physiological capacity to attack invasive medications. Unfortunately, for Tommy, the prednisone had not discriminated between shielding the medication he had been prescribed and safeguarding an infection. The infection in that little boy was winning.

Tommy watched as his new friend walked over to the doctor still battling the rage of a protective mother. All the way there, Tommy could hear Chris mumbling to himself.

"Doctor Rad!"

The little smile had never left Tommy's face.

It can happen that fast. If Chris had arrived at work as scheduled, by the time he got there, Tommy would have already been in the general ward for treatment of pain symptoms. If he had managed to leave the hospital alive, it would have been weeks later, probably without his right leg. But that night Chris was early, and Tommy was still in the emergency room. Chris had seen the strange occurrence before and was able to step in. Tommy was still admitted for the night, but instead of pain management, his treatment was focused on the infection raging in his leg.

* * *

"Don't pull this shit on me!"

Despite their shock from Chris's rare burst of emotion, or perhaps because of it, the ER nurses continued to flawlessly execute their tasks. The only sounds coming from the ER room were Chris's rage and the piercing monotone shriek of the heart monitor as it continued to strain, in search of any target to trace. Old Betty's only contribution that night was trying to muffle the sound of Dr. Baxter's growing frustration.

Chris shot a glance at the clock on the wall. He knew this patient was not coming back, but there were still two more minutes of CPR to administer. One drawback to working within the rigid boundaries of standard operating procedures was the need to endure an extended personal connection to a man he did not know and would not save. Those final two minutes passed by painfully slow as Chris continued the bond. Finally, with his full attention on the face of John Doe, he said goodbye. Chris had lost another friend.

"Call it."

"11:59, Doctor."

There was nothing more to do. John Doe was now officially deceased. All at once, the remaining tenants of the room exhaled a sigh of relief as the walls again pushed out and an almost-blinding white light returned the glory of life, for there was no longer a fight to rescue the dying. Chris removed his latex gloves—clean on the outside yet filled with the sweat of his desperation—tossed them into the waste, then turned to storm out of the room.

"This is what I get for starting my rounds ahead of schedule. Early is on time, on time is late. Bullshit!"

Indeed, early is on time and on time is late. Chris Baxter believed the words, as they never steered him wrong. But, at 11:59 that night, for only the slightest of moments, a flood of doubt crossed his mind before quickly passing. He remained frozen—the time for self-loathing had passed. Everything slipped away except for Chris and John Doe. No other thoughts entered the doctor's mind but his connection to the body below him. Though the nurses were right there, he was no longer aware of them. There were no sounds, or images, nor were any other senses alert, only the tactile sensation of a lifeless body. Chris remained turned away, leaving one hand on the leg of his dear friend as he leaned against the gurney. He closed his eyes and thought of nothing but the comfort of their connection. For someone who spent so much time juggling work, emotions, and flashbacks, finally coming to a rest was indeed a welcome change.

This will not last. His thought broke Chris out of a trance. But he was not yet willing to part with the beautiful instance of peace and serenity. He wondered if John Doe had felt the same way when he arrived. Chris found it hard to imagine he would ever feel such tranquility again.

His thoughts were alive. *This is wonderful. Divine. You could stay here forever, but it's not your time yet.* "Damn," was the only word able to sneak its way past Chris's clenched jaw.

It was definitely going to be one of those weekends.

Chris looked over at Rachel. She stared back with an awkward, forced smile, trying to decide how to break the tension. There was just the slightest hesitation before she shared her thought.

"Well, midnight is here now. Let's hope Saturday skips any death or drama!"

Unsure why, Rachel pulled back, immediately regretting her comment.

II - Saturday, March 29, 2014

BANGKOK, THAILAND

Laksi District

Morning

Silence, as if the entire city had been abandoned years before.

All you had to do, however, was look up to the toll road running high overhead, no more than half a kilometer away, for a reminder: the city was indeed alive, just not on this stretch of road.

No, the street had not been forgotten. In fact, just then, twenty-seven people were preparing to revitalize that part of Bangkok.

Seven vendors were opening their shops, all of them in various stages of preparation. Some held broomsticks, ready to sweep off entryways. Others stood by the day's selection of fresh meats, fish, and vegetables, waiting to fill the market stalls lining the street. All were preparing...waiting...

Four vagrants, dressed in whatever paltry clothing they were able to find, were sitting beside their belongings, grime-stained fingers strumming the ground or picking yesterday's meal from their beards.

One character seemed out of place. A businessman, perhaps, or maybe that's what he was on better days. He seemed to be suffering the effects of Friday night's debauchery, still clutching a near-empty bottle of Mekhong whiskey, vomit running down the front of his cheap suit to his urine-stained trousers.

The rest were teenagers. Fifteen street rats who were either headed to, or coming from, trouble. For the moment, they were just waiting for something to determine the next move for them.

Twenty-seven people were waiting in limbo for the rest of the world to catch up.

Life resumed the moment a black sedan entered from the south. Saturday's first market shoppers would soon have an opportunity to spend their money, give it away, or have it stolen.

After energizing twenty-six of the locals, the car gently pulled over to the side of the road. Two men exited: a Thai Army officer and an American. The officer directed his driver to remain in the vehicle. He looked down at the drunk, slowly shaking his head in pity. With a gentle wave of his hand, he selected the direction to begin their tour.

"Please, come!"

As the two men began to walk the streets of Bangkok, Colonel Seni Chati seemed to be unaware of the dangers lurking around every corner. Maybe unafraid was a better description, for soldiers under his command had already cleared the area in preparation for his visit. Loitering teenagers, homeless tramps, and street peddlers normally filled these bustling city streets, ensuring both commerce and crime were plentiful. Earlier in the day, however, local units of the Royal Thai Army had rounded up the vagrants. Broadcasting through a speaker mounted on one truck, a booming and unsympathetic voice orchestrated the frenzy. As soldiers stormed the streets, the voice instructed in Thai, "All those in the area must board our vehicles immediately. Do not leave the street. Do not enter the buildings. If you are in the buildings, immediately come out." A broken English translation followed before the recording looped back to the start. No other instructions were needed as no one resisted.

Soldiers barked similar commands while they rounded up the people. They were neither forceful nor gentle. They conducted themselves efficiently and carefully, making sure no stragglers were left behind. The trucks left as quickly and unexpectedly as they had arrived. The destination was unknown to the new passengers.

In the emptied space, an equal number of teens, vagrants, beggars, and vendors were moved in to replace those who had just been carted off. This new group looked the same, were just as disheveled, but they were armed and ready to come to the aid of Colonel Seni should the need arise.

The Thai soldiers had conducted this exercise on every street of the four-block downtown area. Three hours later they repeated the exercise, this time returning the civilians and collecting the disguised troops. Between the two disruptions, Colonel Seni conducted his tour of the area. When escorting international guests through the city, Colonel Seni preferred to keep up appearances; he was aware that his country's social welfare status was well known to the world and believed there was no good reason to hide the unsightly appearance. It would only increase speculation and doubt. He didn't want anything to further hinder the support he needed from his American friend.

Scott Gipson was many things, but a friend of Colonel Seni's was not one of them. Walking down the street, he looked every bit the part: a cunning businessman, an entrepreneur exploring the possibility of expanding his company's global presence by moving its Eastern Asian operations to Thailand. But this was only his cover story, one that allowed Colonel Seni to escort Gipson with the circumstance usually given to visiting capitalists. Hosting potential investors was part of the colonel's job, and he often used his army to provide security.

Gipson walked alongside his escort, just as he had for the last three days. He limited his conversation to the occasional question. Mostly, he watched and listened. He didn't take notes or photographs while at any of the sites. Daily debriefings conducted for his superiors would augment the images and recordings already documented throughout every moment of his day.

Gipson's lean build, which seemed perfectly molded to fit his light gray Desmond Merrion suit, did not make him seem submissive or intimidating. He stood taller than the Asian contacts he was introduced to, yet would easily blend in with most Western tourists. What did stand out was his thick red hair and slightly graying beard, neatly groomed but starting to show the wear of the long trip away from home. Scott Gipson mirrored a man interested in money, and in how the people of Thailand could make more for him. Colonel Seni was the only person on the street who knew otherwise.

Colonel Scott Gipson was, in fact, a senior operative with the Special Activities Division of the United States Central Intelligence Agency. He had been working in covert operations for most of his twenty-three-year career with the US Army. Colonel Gipson did not deploy to combat zones. Instead, he and his team went to places where war was brewing. His main objective was defusing or eliminating foreign tensions that were threatening US national interests. When de-escalation was not possible, special forces teams or traditional military units were called in to engage. Outright war was never a preferred result. Colonel Gipson hated failing.

Anger over election tampering and the refusal to engage in needed political reform had increased significantly over the past several months. Just the week before, Thailand's Constitutional Court had declared the recent general election invalid. Turmoil like this was commonplace in Thailand and had been ever since the Siamese Revolution of 1932.

"Colonel Seni, I am going to recommend to my command that there be a formal protest to the United Nations over the Royal Thai Army's disruption of the general election and the Constitutional Court's efforts to maintain the recognized government structure."

Colonel Seni knew his country's political problems did not help matters, yet he was still surprised by Gipson's statement. His plan to send a positive report back to General Prayut was shattered in an instant. "No, no, my friend. But that is not any case. The general assures me that our army is helping the Court with their every need." Colonel Seni's poor grammar was offset by his perfect pronunciation. He spoke with a Midwestern American accent, convincing enough to almost make a stranger think he was just a friendly neighbor chatting about something as benign as the weather. Gipson knew better.

As they continued strolling down the street. Gipson, his thumbs casually hooked on his trouser pockets, began kicking pebbles off to the side of the street. First to the left. The gang of fifteen teenagers separated into three groups and scattered across the block, horsing around and laughing. Then, to the right. The market stands were nearly set up. None of the vendors looked at the

American. Back to the left. The homeless men, who had gathered up and were now carrying their belongings, began to drift in the same direction as the colonel.

Gipson stopped and turned to his guide. "That is clearly *not* the case, Colonel Seni. Every step of this process has been interfered with since the Commission first tried to facilitate this election." Gipson's tone sharpened as the volume of his voice increased. While the disguised soldiers were not close enough to hear the conversation, it was clear their commander was getting a tongue-lashing from the American. The scene unsettled them.

Gipson continued, "There is clear evidence you and your soldiers are backing these anti-government protests. Or, at least, you are not trying to ease the tensions. I asked for this tour today to see the street where the eighteen innocent civilians were killed yesterday. Your men sat back and allowed that situation to escalate until it exploded into gunfire. Your soldiers ended up killing thirteen protestors, people on both sides. How could you allow this to occur?"

"No, that is not what happened," Seni countered. "We tried to allow for peaceful slogan, but when the first rocks were threw, my men were forced to protect each other, and also the innocent people of Bangkok. Our aim was to stop the quarrel. In this, you must agree we were successful. When innocent people are hurt or killed, I always regret that. My goal was to have my men bring back these streets to the people. You can clearly see here that we have succeeded on this."

Colonel Seni extended his arm and fanned it in an arc over the block to proudly show off the miserable conditions of the city. "See how they go about life today? Every Thai is an equal citizen. Without fear! This is the same place as the attack you blame on us. These poor souls were here yesterday. See how we have comforted them? They return without fear. This is a great effort, my friend!" Gipson didn't answer right away and continued walking quietly. He wanted to give Colonel Seni the impression he was considering his frenzied words, maybe even believing them.

Looking around, Scott marveled at the bustling Laksi District, one of Bangkok's wealthiest areas. The most modern office towers and convention centers stood tall between Buddhist temples and architecture dating back to the Kingdom of Siam. There were extravagant parks around the liana, preserving great vines that once canopied the jungle. The city streets were the only separation between old and new Thailand in this district. It was here that great monuments to both eras came together, reminding Thailand's people where they came from as they fought to make their humble homeland a global economy.

Scott also knew it was here in the Laksi District that political protests and anti-government sentiment first took root. Government turmoil had been a constant for over a decade, well before Thailand's prime minister was overthrown in 2006. Since that time, the Red Shirts and Yellow Shirts (pro- and anti-government groups) had more closely resembled football hooligans than organized political groups. Gipson was still unsure which side the Royal Thai Army favored. He was convinced that General Prayut Chan-o-cha, the Thai Army commander, would soon align with one of these groups, or he would break off a new faction. Gipson knew that whatever group he chose, the general would put the full force of his army behind it. He also knew that the fight would start right there in the Laksi District.

Scanning the street, Gipson was keenly aware of the fact that no one was paying attention to him or Colonel Seni. If it wasn't a national day of mourning following yesterday's violence, these streets would be teeming with Saturday market vendors and business executives. Scott knew the "vendors, vagrants, and teens" were prepared to use their weapons, if they had to. He was comforted by the fact that his own soldiers, whose identities were unknown to everyone else in the district, would never give them the opportunity to raise arms.

Colonel Gipson finally decided he had seen and heard all he could stomach. He called for an end to the tour. "This whole situation is a tinderbox, ready to explode at any time. I just hope that General Prayut doesn't use you as his spark, my friend."

PORTLAND, OREGON

John Doe was the last patient to die on Dr. Baxter's shift. Chris welcomed death's reprieve, especially after the-less-than stellar beginning. For the rest of the night and well into Saturday afternoon, no more patients came into the ER. He even managed to sneak about four hours of sleep in between inspecting idle equipment, checking stock levels, and countless trips up and down the empty halls.

A minimally staffed emergency room must always be prepared for the next wave which will inevitably crash, carrying with it the battered bodies of those in need of care.

But the needy never did come to Saint Augustus that Saturday. A garrison built to house personnel and the supplies needed for the fight against illness and death has little value when peace blankets the land. Soldiers grow weary, equipment rusts, provisions become stale.

As Chris roamed the quiet halls, an uneasy feeling came over him. Although the sensation was a familiar one, his surroundings were suddenly unfamiliar. In his past, such a feeling was inevitably a precursor to activity. "Activity," for an Army doctor in a combat zone, meant only one thing: death. Chris had borne witness to that reality too many times to not recognize the signs. This was different, for this time he was home. Chris was back in Portland, where activity was always limited, and the resulting death held to a minimum. Those uneasy feelings should have remained behind on battlefields around the world.

At seven o'clock Saturday evening, it was still quiet at Saint Augustus, as if the hospital was closed and shuttered. Suddenly, a piercing squelch from the radio at the front desk broke the calm with an inbound ambulance notification. Three minutes out. The patient was a fifty-two-year-old woman with chest pains. Baxter's face showed signs of relief, for activity, his unwanted friend, had not yet abandoned him.

Well, we won't make the news tonight with this patient, Chris thought, *but it'll do.*

AROUND THE WORLD

Most of the memories we retain capture moments in our lives when something changed. We tend to hold on to the cherished times when bad turned to good or when good turned into better. We also lament changes for the worse, holding on to them for only as long as we must, using them as reminders to appreciate the things we hold dear.

The absence of death is a moment that may be overlooked altogether, if only for a bit.

* * *

In the sub-Saharan African nation of Mali, rituals of death are well practiced. War, starvation, and disease ensure that death is a constant part of life. There is little time to mourn the dead. In small villages throughout the country, bodies are hastily collected for burning in an ongoing effort to stem the spread of disease. Those who are dying are gathered from their homes and relocated to positions outside the village. There, they wait with their family for death, using the time to pray and share love and sorrow. When death arrives, cremation must occur immediately. Mourning loss is a luxury only the wealthy, with their advanced medicine, can afford. The focus here must instead be on those who live.

By late in the day on Saturday, there were no more bodies to burn. Gathering the dying continued, but none of the journeys would complete.

* * *

When not engaged in direct combat operations, US Marines patrolling the Helmand Province in Afghanistan had only two missions. First, they waited. Captain Benji Torim hated to wait. "If the bullets aren't flying right now, they will be soon."

Too long a wait inevitably led to the second order: patrol the province to find out why no one was shooting. No violence was translated as planning for upcoming bloodshed–and the longer the simmer, the deeper the slash. No one expected peace.

On this particular Saturday, eighteen separate patrols left from forward operating bases across the province. Each patrol was made up of three Humvees carrying six marines, a medic, a military translator, and an Afghan local. The patrols were armed with .50 caliber machine guns mounted on each turret, standard-issue M-16 rifles, as well as radio call signs and signals, to rain down death on any enemy fight within ninety seconds. In Helmand, unfortunately, most engagements were over in sixty—thirty seconds before marines could get help. Hit and run. Every marine knew about this split-second gap.

With eighteen patrols leaving, the over/under was seven skirmishes; every patrol nervously waited to see if they could beat the average. On that Saturday, in the country's most deadly province, no one had the chance to try.

For the first day in years, medic calls were silent.

* * *

In Paris, much like other major cities of the world, news reporters scrambled to cover stories celebrating moments of victory. "Cheated Death!" "Heroic Rescue," and "Brave Samaritan" wrapped each story in its own glorious moment. The oddness of the day was missed by most. Only morgues, churches, and temples noticed the subtle change, as the source of their livelihood was interrupted.

* * *

After a long day at Saint Augustus, after anticipating the worst, all Chris Baxter got was one patient whom he saved with the help of Old Betty. Just enough time remained on his shift to clear his patient out of the ER and send her to recovery. He high-fived his replacement, then strolled out through the front door at twenty minutes after noon on Sunday.

"It's a good day when no one dies!" Chris smiled as he headed to his car.

III - Sunday, March 30, 2014

Details of significance from that Sunday shall forever remain uncharted, mired between the first scenes of a most unusual week and humankind's later reaction. For one day, however, people in different cities, towns, and villages each came to grips with what was, unbeknownst to them, a global anomaly. Unaware there was a pattern, the world spotlighted the brave heroes in these seemingly miraculous events and the good fortunes of the "lucky few" who survived. Some waited in fear for the counterbalance they thought would surely offset that one gloriously peaceful day. Others suffered the agony that comes when death does not make its wonted arrival.

SEOUL, SOUTH KOREA

Korean Air Lines Flight KL019 from Atlanta to Incheon International Airport was originally scheduled to arrive at four thirty-nine in the afternoon, but a late departure from Atlanta, and heavy spring thunderstorms blanketing the Korean peninsula, delayed its arrival by several hours. As the plane rattled its way through turbulent weather, Sarah prayed that her fragile nerves would hold out.

We're almost there. We're almost there.

Sitting in a cramped airplane seat for over fifteen hours was grueling enough, but when the flight time—prominently displayed on the moving map in front of her—surpassed the twenty-hour mark, Sarah knew there had to be a special word in Korean for the trip. She made a mental note to ask her cousin to translate "flight from hell" as soon as she saw him.

The pilot's voice came alive over the intercom. Sarah couldn't understand what he was saying, but from the reactions of other passengers, mainly South Korean nationals returning home, she guessed the news was not good. Being the seasoned international traveler she now was after this marathon trip, she waited for the English translation and braced herself for the bad news. "Hello, ladies and gentlemen. I am sorry to tell you that we have been directed to circle once more to make space for another plane before our final approach to land. This should not add more than fifteen minutes to our flight. Thank you for your patience." News of this latest delay was delivered in the most soothing voice: perfectly pronounced words spoken with a slight British accent. She wondered if the pleasurable tones of her own language were received the same by other passengers, or did they prefer their native tongue? To her, all Korean sounded harsh.

Sarah reached up to the map on the TV screen and traced her finger along the thin red line marking her journey halfway around the globe. She had left everything she knew behind at the beginning of the red track. The other end, her destination, was going to separate her from where she had started in a way much more significant than the thin line suggested. The food. The music. And the language! Its impersonal intonation made it hard for her to distinguish a soft verse of poetry from a menacing threat.

Looking around the cabin, Sarah was no longer in a sea of unfamiliar faces, no longer leaving the States with a plane "full of foreigners." She was going to arrive in South Korea with many of its citizens; Sarah was the alien now. She began to feel the first bit of trepidation since planning for the trip three weeks ago. She had so many questions and so few answers. *Will I be comfortable? Will I like the food? Will I be able to understand anyone?*

As the turbulence subsided, she remembered the reason for her visit, and it was that one thought that quelled most of her fears: Sarah was coming home.

* * *

Sarah Pak was born in South Korea, but she knew little of the country claiming to be her homeland. Born Pak Ji-hyun, but always known as Sarah, she had lived in Korea for less than a month before her parent took her to Atlanta.

Sarah's father, Pak Kun-hee, preferred the name Kyle. Born in Korea, Kyle Pak became an American citizen after choosing to attend Georgia Institute of Technology instead of going to the university in Seoul. He no longer wanted to live in, or even witness, the kind of poverty in which he had been raised. Good fortune smiled on Kyle, and when it did, he left Korea and vowed to never return. Instead, he launched a successful career as a software engineer in his new homeland.

Kyle was a brilliant engineer and developer. Many large technology firms tried to lure him with dazzling salaries, bonuses, and lavish benefits, but their offers did not interest him, at least not those from the companies that wanted to use him as a token liaison to attract South Korean customers and investors with "one of their own."

By refusing these offers, however, Kyle only succeeded in raising his market value. In the end, he could no longer resist them. Making an occasional trip to Asia was worth the millions he earned. The moment he returned to the United States, however, he was able to box up his ancestry until the next Asian business trip.

It was on one of these trips that Kyle met Han Mi-rim, a secretary with one of his client companies. She fell for Kyle immediately. He fell even faster and harder. Her captivating beauty and demeanor ignited devotion to a culture he had long lost the taste for, if it ever existed in the first place. Many of Kyle's preconditions were quickly set aside when he, once again, reached a point where resistance was exhausted.

Han Mi-rim wanted nothing more than to start a new life in America as Mrs. Mary Pak. Her only condition was going home at least twice a year to visit her family. As long as Kyle agreed to this, she would marry him and make sure their life in America remained American: red, white, and blue, apple pie, John Wayne. To Kyle, it was a fair trade; there were definite benefits to making sure his wife was happy.

When she was six months pregnant with their daughter, Mary joined Kyle on a business trip to South Korea. Soon after they arrived in her hometown, Mary grew ill, and would never leave Korea again. Kyle was close by her side when Han Mi-rim died while giving birth to Pak Ji-hyun. Pak Kun-hee organized a traditional seven-day funeral, in glorious honor to the culture his wife had adored. At the end of the shortened mourning period, Kyle packed away what remained of his lost life before he and baby Sarah left, never to return.

* * *

Sarah sat back in her seat and wondered if her mother had hated this flight as much as she did. Probably not, she thought as she chuckled quietly to herself. She was sure her dad always flew on a private plane, or in first class at the very least. Well, Ms. Pak didn't have that option. She was paying for this trip herself.

* * *

His daughter's strength and confidence were the main reasons Kyle agreed to Sarah's trip to Korea for her eighteenth birthday. She was a senior in high school, a straight-A student, scheduled to graduate in June and then attend the University of North Carolina. Kyle was sure she would become a great, as-yet-undetermined something. Kyle wanted her to attend his alma mater, but in Sarah's opinion, it was too close to home, so he agreed to let her put a couple of states between them.

Kyle never returned to Asia after his wife died there. He never left the United States again either, preferring to make his fortune remotely. When Sarah expressed interest in learning to read and write Hangul, Kyle tried to discourage her. When she wanted to explore and learn the Korean culture, he attempted to steer her in other directions. Kyle wanted to forget the life he had left behind there, and he certainly never wanted his daughter to become a part of it. But he lost that fight to a will more stubborn than his own.

He promised to pay for Sarah's college, but then she earned a full academic scholarship. He offered to pay for her housing, but she told him it was unnecessary. Instead, she wanted to use money she had saved up from the weekly allowance he had been giving her for years. Kyle paid for most of her other expenses, but he also expected his daughter to appreciate the value of money. Therefore, he gave her what he considered a meager stipend: $300 a week. Kyle took pride in the way he handled these kinds of first-world concerns. Issues like this were a far cry from what he was used to dealing with when he was growing up.

Despite her father's lavish blanket of protection, Sarah had learned the value of money long ago, saving all she could, spending only when it was absolutely necessary. Her father's investment broker, Sarah's "Uncle" Roy, even set her up with a portfolio. "Slightly aggressive, since I have the advantage of my age, but mostly modest growth," was how she described her investing approach to her father, proudly showing him a balance of over $50,000, a result of her frugal ways and her savings.

Sarah wanted to visit Korea, meet her family, and visit her mother's grave. Her desire far outweighed any argument Kyle could come up with.

* * *

When an announcement blared from the intercom and the passengers let out a Korean version of "hooray!" Sarah knew there would be good news in the English translation that was about to follow. "Ladies and gentlemen, our flight attendants will go about now and prepare the cabin for landing at Incheon International Airport."

Sarah's heart bounded with the thought of meeting her cousin, Bung-ju, for the first time. She had only spoken to him twice, both times just before she made the flight reservation. She had only the fewest details about him, which her father confirmed.

Flight KL019 began its final approach. The lights were brightened, the window shades lifted, but a dreary, occluded sky darkened the cabin. Sarah squirmed, once again second-guessing her decision to fly coach. But nothing could dampen her elation. Tomorrow she would awaken in her homeland, seven thousand miles from home. Over the next week, she would be living in a new world. Thursday, she would turn eighteen in the same house where her mother had turned eighteen. She would finally have a connection to a past she never knew.

As the Airbus 300 was making its final approach, the weather remained a challenge. Stormy winds began to knock the jet around. With near-zero visibility, the pilots relied on the CAT III-b airport, Asia's first. The Instrument Landing System could fly the jet to within ten feet of its target landing spot on the runway.

As Sarah stared through the window, trying to see land, she began to daydream: *I wonder if I'll recognize Bung-ju. I bet he has the same eyes as my mom and my aunt. "Hello, Bung-ju. Yo-bo-say-yo. Yowe-bow-saaay-yo." That sounds better! The first thing I'm going to do tomorrow is visit Mama's grave. I wonder if we'll stay in Seoul today, or go straight to Wonju? I think I want them to call me Pak Ji-hyun.*

The landing was flawless, with the rear tires of the aircraft perfectly splitting the runway. As the pilot guided KL019's nose down, the copilot prepared to reverse thrust on the engines to slow the aircraft. Ji-hyun squealed with excitement. "I'm home, Mama!"

The sudden lunge of the plane while fighting the new direction of the engines was more than its her nose landing gear could bear. With little regard for the one hundred twenty-three lives aboard, a flawed drag brace snapped. Flight KL019 broke apart as it tore across the runway in search of a final resting place.

MT. DEFIANCE, OREGON

Chris Baxter would never take part in the lull facing our world. He was focused on one thing: exiting the city, leaving all the commotion and excitement behind. He craved peaceful isolation. With his pack already loaded in the trunk, Chris had hopped in his car and zipped out of the hospital lot. He reached the trailhead just before the sun began its slow descent to the horizon. An unremarkable sign, staked at the beginning of a path meandering through the trees, simply read, "Mt. Defiance 5.1 mi."

With a steep climb of almost five thousand feet and steady spring rain, he thought it unlikely that other hikers would be on their way up to the snow-covered crest. Any resemblance to city life immediately faded once Chris started up the trail, except the occasional hum of a semi-tractor barreling down the interstate, engine echoing across the cavern walls of the Columbia Gorge. Before long, even those faint sounds disappeared.

Chris loved the seclusion of the mountain. In fact, in his free time, he enjoyed solitude. Except for work colleagues and a few old friends, whom he preferred to keep at a distance, he kept to himself. He had no family; he was the only child of Sam and Linda Baxter, who were both only children of only children of only children, for as far back as anyone could recall.

Chris lived his life to help others. He was able to fulfill this goal by treating patients in the hospital, and by volunteering his time to work with the young people in his community. Their yearning for care was like a narcotic to him. But there's only so much a person can give before they require a respite. For Chris, this respite was solitude and the chance to clear his mind and soul. For one night, Chris had nothing to do but climb.

A small, unimproved dirt path wound into the forest until it vanished. In its place stood the mountain. Gentle waterfalls and streams broke up the mossy background of rock and evergreens, showcasing every hue of green and brown the earth created. At a pace nearing a full sprint, he navigated the trail without pausing to marvel at the enchantment of his ever-changing surroundings.

All at once, the route turned straight into Defiance as if to proclaim, "It's time to climb now." Chris started up, keeping his eyes down, carefully watching his placement of each foot on the uneven ground. On Defiance, the zigzag of switchbacks extended the trail to over five miles but reduced the extreme ledge of the mountain to that of a steep, rocky hill. For Chris, hiking was a sport that kept his body in excellent condition while giving him a chance to focus on nothing but the placement of each step and his controlled, rhythmic breathing. After reaching the snow-covered crest in fifty-two minutes, a personal best, Chris set up his campsite, relishing the civilian life he now lived. It felt good not to have to worry about securing his position from the enemy, and instead only having to protect from nature's wind and snow. Finally leaning back on his pack to watch the setting sun, Chris reflected, "Life will never get better than this. Right here, right now."

PORTLAND, OREGON

It was a reporter from the *Portland Times* who made the first connection in this strange puzzle.

She had been trying to write a story that she hoped would be selected as the week's "Links to Portland's Past" spotlight article. After a few years at the *Times*, reporting on bland stories about small-town Portland lost the allure it once held; she wanted to write something more profound—a heartfelt story for all ages, perhaps a gripping exposé on a "love once lost," or maybe publishing an article like that would help her get a job writing for a national publication. All she needed was a story so good it would write itself.

She looked everywhere for inspiration, finding nothing of interest in the police blotters or the weekly summaries of events at local hospitals and firehouses. Trying to find a national story buried among twelve house fires, three dog bites, and sixteen bicycle and car accidents was pointless. *Maybe another account of the growing meth lab problem and maybe tying that to recent fires? Perhaps another piece on the battle between bikes and cars in Portland?* No. She knew what the response from readers would be: "If I have to read one more goddamn story about whatever goddamn story it is this time, I'm going to kill someone!" She did not want to become another reporter whose career died after writing the same piece one too many times. After seven hours searching she was convinced that the week of March 22 to 28 would go down in the record books as Portland's most boring week ever. Everything was a dead end.

On the last page of the appendix for the townships just outside the city limits, she read about a death at Saint Augustus Hospital. Something about it seemed familiar. She read the blotter entry aloud.

> March 28, 2014. Saint Augustus Hospital, Portland, Oregon. Unidentified white male, age unknown, estimate 25-40 years old. Unresponsive when brought in. Time of record 23:59 local. No complaint filed. Cause of death: Unknown. Pending further investigation. Christopher J. Baxter, MD, FACEP, FAAEM.

After two more hours of searching through the *Times* archives, a headline from 1986–"Mysterious Body Identified"–caught her eye. The story was about a Portland-area native, Samuel Baxter, and the circumstances surrounding his death. As she read the article, she glanced at the 2014 blotter from the same date. Same name, Baxter, was the attending. It didn't take much to connect Dr. Christopher Baxter of 2014 to the little Chris Baxter from 1986.

"Bingo!" The reporter leaned back, convinced there was an interesting connection that warranted a phone call first thing Monday morning.

IV - Monday, March 31, 2014

MT. DEFIANCE, OREGON

Morning

Waking well before sunrise, Chris basked in the solitude of the morning despite harsh conditions on the mountain. The temperature had remained well below freezing all night, and there was a fresh three-inch layer of snow and ice everywhere. Defiance remained the sanctuary he was hoping to reunite with. While sipping his third cup of coffee, snacking on some trail food, Chris soaked in the last peaceful moments of the new day's entrance before traversing the easygoing terrain on his way down to the trailhead. This time, Chris took the time to enjoy every fabulous view he encountered. His world changed with every step, starting off with a crystal-clear view atop the packed ice, but by the time he was below the snow line, rising temperatures transformed the area into a damp, overcast scene.

After fifteen hours immersed in the raw beauty of the mountain, Chris was ready to resume his regular life. Upon reaching the trailhead, he got to his car, tossed his pack in the trunk, and turned on his cell phone. His mind was already racing, planning, and organizing the upcoming week. For most of the drive home, he thought about his highest priority, John Doe, and what he needed to do. Lost in thought, he jumped when the call came in.

“Hello?”

“Dr. Baxter? Is this Dr. Christopher Baxter?”

“Speaking.”

“Dr. Baxter, this is Colleen Fellow from the *Portland Times.* I was looking over the metro hospital logs from this weekend. You were the attending emergency room doctor at Saint Augustus Hospital over the weekend, correct?”

“Correct.” Chris had fielded hundreds of calls from reporters in the past who were looking for a scoop on some shooting or accident. He knew what she was after. But if she was going to be asking about John Doe, he didn’t have any answers for her. He didn’t have the answers himself, and he definitely wasn’t about to give this eager columnist the list of possibilities he was considering.

“Doctor, I’ll get right to the point. The circumstances around the death of a patient are exactly the same circumstances as the death of your father, Samuel Baxter–”

"Sam," Chris interrupted. "Sam Baxter."

"Sorry, Sam Baxter. I'm sure you're aware of the connection to your father's death."

"Indeed, I am." He didn't know why he chose to answer that way. It hadn't even occurred to him that there was a connection. Chris's thoughts drifted back to the events surrounding his father's death. It was a part of his life he had let go of long ago. The memories remained, but he was no longer their captive.

"I'm not sure if you remember me. I wrote a profile piece on you for Portland's 9/11 celebration a while back."

"I remember, Colleen. It was hardly a celebration." For the moment, he was unwilling to offer more, delaying the conversation with small talk while he revisited the details of the Sam Baxter story. Chris assumed control of the call and was going to set its pace.

"Sorry, poor word. For the memorial."

"Remembrance."

"Right. Sorry. For the remembrance. I profiled you back then. We never talked, but my research showed that your father passed away in the emergency room in 1986. That was why you came back there, 'to continue service the way my dad wanted' was what you said at the remembrance, I believe."

Chris then used a tactic he had perfected years earlier when interviewed about returning to Portland after his military career: he dished out a few personal details. "That's right. Officer Sam Baxter served with the Beaverton Police Department admirably for fifteen years. He benefited his community before, during, and after his time on the force. It has always been my commitment to serve like he did. I wanted to come back and work here, to continue my service where my father's ended." A childish sense of satisfaction came over him, capped off with a grin that pulled his left cheek tight. *Every time I play this role, they eat it up.*

"That's touching, Dr. Baxter."

"Chris."

"Chris. That is indeed admirable. I was just reaching out to see if you find the similarities between the two deaths odd."

Their discussion was beginning to touch on topics that were too close, too personal for him. Chris turned off the highway onto the exit ramp, figuring they would wrap up just as he pulled into his driveway. "Odd? I'm not sure about odd. It's just a random coincidence. Many people die in the Saint Augustus ER. At some point, there are going to be two people who die from unexplained circumstances in the same ER. The fact that the two events occurred is actually very probable." Chris was intent on embarrassing her for intruding in his life.

"I'd have to agree with you about that, I guess."

"Yes, and the fact that the attending physician who unsuccessfully tried to resuscitate one of those unexplained deaths is the now-grown son of the other unexplained death is just another statistically probable occurrence."

"That's right." Colleen began to feel as if the conversation wasn't going anywhere. Listening as Chris spewed everything aloud just made her probe sound foolish. She correctly felt he was just toying with her now.

"If all of those events are nothing out of the ordinary, then coding in the same triage room is no longer a stretch now, is it?"

"Nope. I guess not."

Chris arrived home just when he thought he would. "Now, the fact that they both died on Friday, March 28 is weird. I have to give you that."

"What?" Colleen Fellow scrambled through her notes in an attempt to confirm the new twist.

Playing cat and mouse with the reporter was fun...for a while, but Chris grew tired of talking to her. Early in the call, he could tell what she knew, what she had already pieced together, and what had never even crossed her mind. He wasn't sure why he gave her the gift of the date connection. If she ever published the limited information she had, even if she didn't see the connection, sooner or later, someone would.

"Listen, Ms. Fellow. I've just pulled into my driveway after a long hike out in the Gorge. Maybe you can call back some other time if my report is not sufficient."

"Sure, we can do that. When–"

Chris didn't wait for the next question. "Great. Thanks, Ms. Fellow. Goodbye."

Dr. Christopher Baxter severely underestimated the effect his conversation with Colleen Fellow from the *Portland Times* would have.

Evening

For the remainder of the day, Chris combed through medical textbooks and journals researching various unexplained causes of death. John Doe's case troubled him. He walked himself through the whole incident, remembering and questioning every step he had taken. *Should I have initiated containment procedures Saturday morning? No. The blood tests came back negative, so there was no need. Maybe the tests run in the San Antonio lab will find something, some cause, something contributing to his death. Hell, I'd be happy if they just found something to put on the death certificate other than "undetermined." Undetermined is such a shitty word.* If a cause of death were discovered, Chris he would revise the death certificate he had filed on Saturday.

While Chris knew that inexplicable deaths could generate a lot of interest in the medical community, and that finding a cause for such a death could be a career-defining discovery for him, his focus now was finding an explanation for John Doe's death. And, of course, he had to find out who John Doe was.

"Undetermined" on a death certificate could have many meanings. Sometimes, it indicated that a doctor, coroner, medic, or medical examiner was unable to conclude how someone died. "Undetermined" is sometimes an easier way to document what "no one wants to say." In some instances, it may be too expensive or time-consuming to determine the actual cause of death. Why did a vagrant sleeping in an alley die? Was it the liquor's long-term effect on his liver, did he freeze to death, or did his heart give out? A corner may find no value in counting all the needle tracks on a filthy, bloated corpse. Was it a drug overdose or a fatal infection? These kinds of deaths could often attract unwanted political attention. These kinds of cases were often left pending.

"Undetermined" may help a family with insurance matters. In trying times, "undetermined" is sometimes a more compassionate cause of death for those left behind, even when they already know the truth.

The undetermined cause of death listed on John Doe's death certificate weighed heavily on Chris. He felt as if he was being lazy, and even uncaring, if he didn't try to figure out what led to the man's death.

These were Chris's thoughts as he reached into his office closet for the folder on his father's death. He was troubled by the haphazard summary of the man's death and life. Chris wondered if his need to determine why John Doe died would be less intense if he hadn't struggled with his father's "undetermined" justification. He dismissed the thought, admitting there was neither a way nor a reason to lessen his drive. Understanding his past could have even sharpened Chris's compassion as a doctor. He imagined knowing the circumstances of his father's death and understanding how some other physician toiled over his dad, how they ran every test twice, reviewed the records over again and studied every part of Sam Baxter's lifeless body until the answer finally popped to the surface.

If Chris found out that his father had killed himself, he would at least have an answer. He would have preferred "suicide" to "we don't know." If it were discovered that Sam Baxter's death had been caused by an as-yet-undiscovered disease, the determination would at least benefit others. "Baxter's disease" would have been a better legacy for a man to leave his son than "undetermined."

Chris could not let another patient's death go undetermined, leaving a family without the knowledge and closure they deserved. Yes, he had every reason to discover John Doe's cause of death.

Chris knew exactly when his own dad had died, and where. What he didn't know was how or why.

PORTLAND, OREGON

Friday, March 28, 1986

Just before midnight, Sam Baxter walked into the emergency room at Saint Augustus Hospital and collapsed. No one ever discovered why, or at least no one ever offered an explanation to the Baxter family. In fact, he was a John Doe until a full week later when they finally identified his body. He had no identification on him. When police ran his fingerprints, nothing came up. There had to be something.

Investigators couldn't get a single lead. They knew he didn't drive to the ER that night, for an unclaimed car was not found on the grounds. There had been no cab fares to the hospital for six hours before he walked in. They talked with the bus drivers who were on duty and only got, "No, didn't notice a quiet, middle-aged white guy on board." So, who was John Doe and where did he come from? No one had an answer.

And no one knew why he died either. He tested negative for everything, showing no signs of illness. There were whispers and concerns that maybe he died of some sort of a mysterious virus or

AIDS, which was a full-blown epidemic in the United States at the time, but those reasons were soon ruled out. The hospital was quick to work with the county sheriff, city police, and health examiners from the state to quell rumors.

On April 5, 1986, after a week of no new information, a clerk from the Washington County Sheriff's Office reran prints for their John Doe. It gave her a reason to "go to the other building." Twenty-five minutes after her smoke break, she bolted into the undersheriff's office.

"Jack, we got a match."

"A match on what?"

"Our John Doe from Saint Augustus. We got a match. He's a...was a cop."

"What?"

"Yeah. A cop with the Beaverton PD. Sam Baxter. He retired a few years ago."

"Why the hell didn't they notify us?"

"I don't know, Jack. I just got back from the other building."

The Beaverton Police Department maintained a shared jurisdiction of Saint Augustus Hospital. They should have been able to identify Sam Baxter's body immediately. They had his fingerprints on file. They even had a blood sample, from an early build and test of the national DNA database. Plus, more than half the force had worked with Sam. His photo had been posted in every squad room, every office, and sketched on the front page of newspapers across the Northwest.

Confirmations and identifications suddenly came pouring in from every channel.

"Yeah, that's Sam Baxter. Wow! I can't believe we missed that."

Everyone confirmed the body as Sam Baxter, a retired sergeant with the Beaverton PD. No one could explain how they had missed the identification before. Visual IDs, fingerprints, blood match, DNA. All tests positively identified Sam Baxter. Friends and relatives looked at the drawings previously released to the public, and at the pictures sent to every agency. They all identified Sam immediately, yet no one could explain why they had missed him before.

Nobody had missed Sam because nobody knew he was missing. Sam and Linda had been divorced for six years by then, and they would often go for weeks without contact. They only spoke when they needed to talk about their son, Chris, who was nearing the end of his junior year in high school.

Chris's days were about girls, the start of baseball season, and planning his last summer adventures. By the fall, life would be all about college applications and dreaming of an escape to the "better life" every teen searches for. The fact that Chris hadn't talked to his dad for over a week was nothing unusual. Not being there when his dad died, not appreciating the significance of the date—that would haunt Chris for years to come.

GLOBAL

How long would it take for you to realize that no one was dying?

Across the globe, connections were starting to take form, as tales of miracles, phenomena, and other extraordinary events were no longer unique.

Credit would never go to one person for recognizing a pattern. Seemingly simultaneous internet postings emerged, each earning its moment in the spotlight when it went viral. No single story took precedence over another, beyond local interest in the city in which it was written. The stories about each local "miracle day" on Saturday led to the same question: "Did it happen again on Sunday?"

Mirroring stories led to the mirror questions around the world:

"Where else did this happen?"

"When did it start?"

"When will it end?"

"Why?"

Answers to these questions would soon begin to unfold. Each would reveal their truth slowly, waiting patiently for their turn in the spotlight, until every question would finally have an answer.

Almost every question.

V - Tuesday, April 1, 2014

PORTLAND, OREGON

Morning

The beginning of a month starts a time like no other in government offices across the United States. For Jodi, an assistant in the Portland City Clerk's office, her focus turns to the past for a day or two. During that time, she is not concerned about today or what may happen tomorrow. Last month, and all of its dry details and comparison to the months preceding, are the only events to consider.

Detailed reports come in from police departments, firehouses, and hospitals, each containing vital statistics on births, marriages, civil unions, and deaths. Names, faces, and personalities of residents are wiped away by the touch of a single office assistant. Jodi determines who might be remembered versus who is merely rolled up into the cold report and forgotten as they're transformed into statistics and summaries. Summaries are then swallowed up to simply become trends. Red arrows pointing up, green arrows nosing down, and arrows lying sideways indicate the data a city has deemed worthy for measuring, but not detailing.

Reported Crime: up ↑ 0.5% (red)

Violent Crime: down ↓ 2.1% (green)

Domestic Violence: up ↑ 1% (red)

Reported Fires: down ↓ 3.0% (green)

Crime-Related: up ↑ 3.4% (red)

While the names of people associated with the tracked data are usually deleted, every now and then, one or two are retained and end up in Jodi's monthly summary. Those names become valuable information, remembered by officials and politicians when they recall, praise, or lay blame to the trends occurring in their city. Those names become part of the means used to define the city for that month, and to grade officials on the quality of their performance serving the citizens.

April 1, 2014 was the same as every other month...

Jodi loved the work she did. It was a responsibility she never took lightly. Accurately gathering data, monitoring trends, and including the right details in her reports could bolster Portland's officials in the eyes of citizens; that is, if the numbers supported campaign promises. The monthly status reports Jodi submitted included all of the details she knew her beloved mayor would want to have.

On that first of the month, Jodi came into the office early, as always, and ready to get to work. Between reports from graveyard staff throughout the city and the never-ending pile of updates, there were mountains of data for her to sift through.

"Good morning, everyone!" Jodi boisterously announced her presence to the empty room; the greeting was simply her moment of charm before solitude commenced. She snapped on the lights and headed straight for the break area to unpack her nourishment for the day.

Though the monthly report rarely took her longer than two days to prepare, presenting a masterpiece of data analysis to her boss before the first day's end was always Jodi's goal and a point of pride for her. Her coworkers at the clerk's office knew the routine and made a point not to interrupt her, especially since they knew distracting her would irritate the commissioner and, consequently, the mayor.

After putting her lunch in the refrigerator and brewing a pot of coffee, Jodi headed to her office. She put her coffee on her desk, sat down, and turned to the computer screen. "Alright, Portland. What stories do you have for me this month?"

Fifteen of twenty-six police precincts had already submitted their reports and nine of the thirteen firehouses came in before another person entered the office. By lunchtime, five of the eleven hospitals had submitted theirs. She also had reports from the City Coroner, Land Assessment, the Water Bureau, Power Bureau, and Department of Sanitation. As the reports continued to come in, Jodi boasted, "As long as those slackers in Station 12 don't drag their feet, this is going to be a piece of cake!"

PACIFIC OCEAN
Flight Level 350
Early Morning

Kyle Pak boarded the charter jet after receiving a call notifying him of the crash. After the airline notification, he made two calls. First, to his assistant. Kyle provided minimal instruction: prepare logistics for an immediate flight to Korea. That was all he needed in order to move.

The next call was to Uncle Roy. "Buddy, there's been an accident with Sarah. I'm leaving in twenty minutes to fly there. Can you come?"

"I'll be outside in five. Just have the car swing by." That was all he needed in order to move. Roy Douglas knew anything involving Sarah was paramount. Where are we going? What happened? Is Sarah okay? The questions could wait; he would surely have all the answers soon. All he needed to do at four thirty in the morning was get dressed, grab his case, and stand outside.

While Kyle mumbled a few words before boarding, once in the air, he didn't speak to anyone for eight full hours. Instead, he was lost in technology. Until he made it to Seoul University Hospital and held her hand, the only link he had to his daughter was digital. For now, all he knew was that she was in a coma, her right leg had been amputated below the knee, and she was currently undergoing a second surgery to try to salvage the fragments of life remaining. Medical personnel were treating the injured, and airline staff members were unable or unwilling to give information to the contact of record beyond the basic confirmation of the accident.

News stories of the crash and aftermath were overwhelming. Stories on television and on the Internet rapidly filled the information gap with rumors, unqualified third-party assumptions, and interviews with emotionally fragile family members grappling to learn the fate of their loved ones. Pieces of information were scrounged together by Roy and Kyle's assistant before sharing. Kyle could not bear wails of loss or guesses by the media as to just how horrible the scene they witnessed was, even as it continued to unfold. If gathered facts were considered worthy, they were passed on, only interrupting Kyle's own research with the shortest of summations regarding their presentation.

Early reports across aviation-buff websites faulted a material failure in the main fitting of the plane's nose landing gear. Grainy video from security cameras appeared to confirm this suspicion. Once the plane had departed from Atlanta and was in the air, nothing could have prevented the tragedy.

South Korea was spared the deadly consequences expected of such a crash. This was due in large part to the technology at Incheon, Asia's most modern airport, and the skills of a well-seasoned aircrew. Kyle reviewed sketches of the airport that diagrammed the crash. The Airbus hit straight on, with little side slip, early into the runway. It managed to slide over ten thousand feet, nearly the full length of the airstrip, before coming to a complete stop, ultimately resisting the urge to plow into the Yellow Sea. Kyle made a note to thank the pilots—or praise them to their next of kin.

There wasn't the fantastic eruption of flames typical in crashes of this magnitude. For flight KL019, basic physics prevailed. Ignition always needs three things: fuel, air, and friction. There was definitely no shortage of friction on landing. In the darkening skies of early evening, sparks careened down the runway. For several hours, Kyle watched videos of the landing, only tearing his eyes away for a moment when Roy interrupted with a new perspective he had uncovered. Both men held their breath as they watched, marveling as the videos were bleached out by the bright glow of sparks. Luckily, the extra hours that flight KL019 spent in the air had drained most of the fuel before impact.

KL019 was not made to survive an event like that. Instead, the plane was designed to sacrifice itself so passengers would have a chance. The wings broke apart, distancing fuel from people. The cabin section had burn-through-resistant thermal and acoustic insulation, providing four minutes of protection for survivors. Four minutes was enough time for a response from the Incheon crash rescue team. Nothing, however, would prepare them for the devastation they saw once they arrived. All one hundred twenty-three occupants, both passengers and crew were alive. Most were still conscious, some writhing in pain. Others were frantically trying to get out of the plane. For those able to free themselves from their seats, getting out was easy, as less than two feet separated their cabin from the runway. The rest of KL019 was littered across the thousands of feet behind it, marking its landing with shredded fuselage and luggage. The air was foul, mixed with a lingering sweet combination of fuel and oil and the scorched remains of wreckage. Out on the runway and inside the plane, children wailed uncontrollably. One young girl frantically tried to wake her mother, undeterred by the blood covering both.

Two-and-a-half hours would pass before all passengers exited or were carried out of the plane. Sarah was the last passenger off the plane, pulled from between the twisted rows of seats that were buried underneath carry-on bags and other debris. Her near-lifeless body was carefully passed from one rescue worker to another until finally it was placed on a stretcher. One final ambulance sped off for the hospital, with sirens blasting. Sarah never got the chance to enjoy the breathtaking night sky of her home country.

No other updates would reach Kyle until he arrived at the hospital. There was nothing else to do but wait and worry. His little girl had grown up a long time ago and he no longer needed to take care of her. All he could do now was wait and pray.

The pilot's voice broke Kyle out of his thoughts. "If you gentlemen could please ensure you are buckled in. We're about to start our descent into Incheon."

PORTLAND, OREGON

Afternoon

Shortly before one o'clock p.m., Jodi finished entering the data from every municipal department in all of Portland's districts and unincorporated zones. As always, she had been careful to follow protocol: first enter the numbers, then translate. Any deviation from this step-by-step method could shape the data to fit a preconceived notion. After a previous mayor had fallen victim to such an error from just this type of mistake nineteen years ago, Jodi was promoted to fill the just-vacant analyst role. Never again was there doubt that the data were properly entered.

* * *

As the strange events happening worldwide were in the process of creating a new reality, Chris was struggling to find a way to sever the perceived link between John Doe and Sam Baxter. It anguished him to think that John Doe's family, whoever they were, would end up inheriting the millstone he himself had carried for so long.

CHRIS BAXTER: BACKSTORY

Chris often reminisced about the date of his father's death. He always held March 28th close to his heart. The date was his own memorial, a justification for detaching from others, instead focusing on brooding and drinking to excess.

Years prior, in 1997, when he was finishing up his first year of residency at Fitzsimons Army Medical Center in Aurora, Colorado, the 28th of March fell on a Friday for the first time since 1986. Chris always held this date close, not out of superstition or because he believed there was a fateful component to it, but because, to him, there was something especially significant about the occurrence of fate in an otherwise random world.

That Friday evening in 1997, Chris walked into his neighborhood bar in Denver. Even though Fitzsimons was scheduled to close down before he applied to its residency program, they accepted him anyway. He often seemed to get what he wanted. Those who didn't know Captain Baxter well thought he was one of the luckiest men alive. Chris stayed at Fitzsimons until it was shuttered, practically turning off the lights when he left.

On Friday, March 28, 1997, none of those issues mattered. Chris walked into the EastTop Saloon, drank Bacardi and Diet Coke mixes for precisely two hours, then closed out every open tab in the bar. When Chris first walked in, he had chatted with the bartender. "For the next couple of hours, put all drinks on my card. Please don't tell anyone. If they leave before me, just tell them someone covered it already. Today's a special day."

It was Chris's solemn remembrance of a private date. One hundred eighty-five people celebrated with Chris that night, paying tribute to a man who never got to see who his son had become. One hundred eighty-five people celebrated, but only two knew it–and a bartender never spills secrets.

Each year, the memories resurfaced, fresh and renewed as if March 28, 1986 was only yesterday. Each year, the same memories would gradually fade and wither until the twenty-eighth rolled around again. As years went by, though, the painful memories slowly began to weaken. They never disappeared entirely, but their shock and surprise gradually wore off.

Working in the same place in which Sam Baxter had taken his last breath never bothered Chris. In fact, when his obligations to the Army were up, Saint Augustus was the only place he wanted to be. Lieutenant Colonel Christopher Baxter served on active duty for a full twenty years. His official retirement was May 31, 2011, a date of no significance.

Logging rounds in an emergency room was hardly the career progression one would have expected from a doctor with Chris's background: West Point graduate, retired lieutenant colonel, combat veteran specializing in field trauma.

Chris was with the US Army's 5th Special Forces Group when they invaded Afghanistan in October 2001. From the minute Chris's mother found out about his deployment, she never stopped worrying. Major Baxter never told her how he was already in

Afghanistan when the Group arrived, preceding them with the CIA's Special Activities Division. Linda Baxter was always proud of her son's accomplishments, but there were still some things she didn't need to fret about. There were always plenty of other chances for her to worry.

Throughout his career, Chris never slowed his pace. Although he was a doctor in the Army Medical Corps, he still managed to train for the Combat Arms: Infantry Basic and Advanced Courses, Airborne, Air Assault, SERE Training (Survival, Evasion, Resistance, Escape). If he was going to work with ground troops, he wanted to train like they trained and know what they knew.

The constant remembrance of his father's death deeply affected Chris. It never slowed or overwhelmed him, but it often shaped his goals. Plans for the future were always somehow linked to Friday, March 28. It guided him into the military, to help save us all from unknown dangers. It led him to medical school, to save humankind from whatever was trying to kill them.

On Friday, March 28, 2003, it drove him to volunteer for assignment in Hong Kong as part of a World Health Organization multinational effort to battle the SARS outbreak in Asia. He knew going to Hong Kong would mean missing out on the invasion of Iraq. In Iraq, however, Chris knew how people would die; he knew how they could be treated. Hong Kong had a lot of Sam Baxters who needed his help.

VI - Wednesday, April 2, 2014

PORTLAND, OREGON

City Hall

It was Wednesday morning when the pieces of this puzzle framed their first silhouette.

Commissioner Philip Cassidy arrived at City Hall much earlier than usual. Even though he and Jodi had already discussed the March report on the phone, he wanted to see the numbers for himself. After she reiterated the summary to her boss, he read through the report, then went through it again. Afterward, they sat quietly in the mayor's office, waiting for him to arrive. Jodi slowly inched her chair closer to the mayor's desk, anticipating the need to defend the accuracy of her report, should someone think she had made an error. She had been doing this job long enough to know her report was highly unusual, that it was going to cause a stir, and she knew her work was impeccable.

When the mayor walked in, Cassidy jumped up and took the lead. "Mayor Teller! There is something you need to be aware of."

Teller shook his head; nothing good ever comes from such a dire greeting.

Both sat in silence and waited for Mayor Teller to absorb the information. He didn't make it past the cover sheet.

"Jesus, this is just like all the other cities we're hearing about. When did this start? When did the last person die?"

"Some John Doe out at Saint A's. Friday night, I think the blotter said. The guy just walked into the emergency room and collapsed."

"Who was he, Philip?" Teller asked as he thumbed through the report.

"No idea. He didn't have any ID on him. And, there is no one matching his description in Portland." Jodi handed the mayor a printout of all the missing-person reports.

"Multnomah County?" Teller asked.

"Nope. Washington...Clackamas...nothing. He looked clean, well dressed, well groomed. No drugs or alcohol in his system."

"Did he say anything?" asked the mayor. The commissioner was at a loss. He looked over to Jodi for help.

"I don't think so," she jumped in. Jodi fumbled through her stack of printouts and manila folders. "None of the reports mention anything," Jodi said as she wrestled through the pages. "The doc said he just walked in and dropped."

"Who was the doctor?"

"Some guy—Baxter, I think." She found the one sheet needed. "Christopher Baxter is what it says here."

"Baxter? Sam Baxter's kid? That's odd, don't you think?"

"I don't know, sir. Who's Sam Baxter?"

Without answering, Mayor Teller called out for his secretary: "Hey, Debbie, can you please get me Sheriff Coleman on the line?"

Michael Teller and Sam Baxter had been friends since childhood. He had known Chris since he was born. In fact, when Chris first came back to Portland, he had asked him to be the guest of honor at the city's ten-year remembrance of 9/11. Teller knew the Baxter family history and was convinced there was more to this story than the sparse details in Jodi's report.

It wasn't until 9:30 a.m. that a staff member picked up the copy of Wednesday's *Portland Times* and glanced at the "Links to Portland's Past" section. It included a collage of photographs of

Saint A's Hospital, Officer Sam Baxter, and Christopher Baxter, MD.

Debbie yelled, "Mr. Mayor, you really need to see this."

Nothing good ever comes from such a dire greeting.

The Portland Times

Links to Portland's Past
by Colleen Fellow

Spring has definitely sprung all around Stumptown! As Portland emerges from yet another sodden winter slumber, a most spectacular natural phenomenon is gripping our city. It has been six years since rhododendrons and azaleas have burst into bloom this early. To my readers loyal to the rose, I express sincere apologies, for you must still wait a few more months. Until the Rose Festival, my city's heart will remain captivated by the vibrant hues and sweet aroma of blooming rhododendrons.

As I was walking along the Crystal Springs Rhododendron Garden yesterday, I found myself lulled back to childhood years by the bright reds, yellows, and pinks marking my way. My mother and I strolled this same pathway so long ago, stopping to smell every blooming shrub and gaze across the waving array of petals. It was there that my mother taught me lessons I still hold dear today: in a rhododendron, purple flows seamlessly into lavender. Pink into rose, then fuchsia. Their colors and shades are fiercely independent, yet it is hard to detect where one ends and the other begins.

I cherished my time in the garden with Mom. With a new story for every rhododendron along the way, we rarely finished the trail before closing time. Dawn to dusk was just never enough time to make it through. Picking up where we left off the day before just did not suffice, as too much would change overnight to not insist on starting over from the beginning.

It was during the walks through the Rhododendron Garden in April, May, and June that I learned about my family. Mom had a story for every flower, every shade telling the tale of a different family member. Dad's memories were always the striking orange blooms. When we passed clusters of orange, his favorite color always stopped us in our tracks. We lost Dad when I was young, so my memories paled in comparison to the stories she conjured up on our walks through the garden.

It was on one of these early spring walks when Mom told me the story of the only time she saw Dad cry. He had recently lost an old friend and was gripped by guilt for not being there in his friend's time of need. They had drifted apart years earlier and Dad never got a chance to say goodbye to Sam. By the time he learned of his buddy's death, the city was already consumed with stories and rumors of Sam Baxter. To protect himself from being associated with Sam during the ensuing frenzy, Dad kept their friendship a secret. Later, he was ashamed that he had allowed fear to dictate his actions.

My mother and father had meandered through the garden, pushing me in my stroller. Mom said it was the first and only time Dad had talked freely about his pal, Sam. Every following year, on the day of Sam's death, amid all the other March 28th celebrations in the Fellow household, Dad would take a walk by himself to remember his friend. Mother always said his swollen red eyes failed to conceal what he tried to hide in the garden.

I had the privilege of speaking with Sam's son, Dr. Christopher Baxter, earlier this week. Surely Chris would have made his father proud. Today, this man—a graduate of the United States Military Academy, who served a career in the US Army, the son of an inexplicable piece of Portland's history—serves our community as a doctor at Saint Augustus Hospital. Dr. Baxter's service is indeed a noble tribute: "to continue my service where my father's ended," is his pledge to our community.

Where and when did Sam Baxter's service end? And how is Chris continuing his father's vision? This past Friday night, twenty-eight years to the day his own father passed, Dr. Baxter was on call at Saint Augustus when an unidentified man died in the emergency room in a way that bears shocking similarities to the death of Sam Baxter.

This tale, however, is not over. This John Doe is on record as the last man to die in Portland. Some rudimentary outreach seems to show him as the last person to die anywhere.

As I walked along the path of the Crystal Springs last night, admiring the multitude of orange rhododendrons, I grieved at the thought that Friday, March 28 might become an indelible Link to Portland's Past.

I wrote my story three times, deleting the pages after each effort. In the end, it was one memory that pulled these words out from me. My father let fear and frenzy suppress his emotions; he regretted it for the rest of his life. I, for one, prefer to not fall victim to another Baxter-tainted *rara avis.*

Some memories of Portland's past are best suited to remain there.

And so, for another day, my friends, I whisper fond blessings to my beloved city. Good night.

~ Colleen

Chris Baxter's Residence

Evening

Chris was finally home for the evening. He was trying to get his head around the interrogation he had just endured—that's exactly what it felt like, an interrogation. He turned on the TV and flipped through the channels. *How am I supposed to know who the hell John Doe was?* As he gazed at the screen, regular programming was interrupted to air an unscheduled press conference with the president.

Chris was deep in thought and yet captivated by the voices interrupting his world.

City Hall

Earlier in the Day

Chris knew it was pointless to interrupt or correct them. They were nervous men on a fishing expedition, clearly determined to uncover Chris's part in all this—whatever "this" was. The *Portland Times* article that created a link to the as-yet-unexplained emergency room death and Chris and Sam Baxter hit the Internet late Tuesday evening, and newsstands by early Wednesday. By 11 a.m., Sheriff Coleman managed to track down Chris as he was heading in to the hospital. Chris would never make it to work that day, informed that his schedule had already been "freed up" for him to have a chat. It had taken the police five days to connect John Doe's death on Friday evening to Sam Baxter, then to realize the two men were linked by Saint Augustus and by March 28th—and that Chris Baxter was connected to both men.

The police weren't sure what to make of any of it. They didn't know how Chris was connected to the crime, what the crime was, or if a crime had even been committed. They were nervous and looking for someone to blame. As they struggled feverishly to uncover more information and to determine if what was going on was simply a matter of coincidence or if it pointed to something far more profound, Chris's frustration mounted.

Chris was seated on one side of the long table, across from a small army of random government officials and law enforcement officers from the metro region. A video camera was trained on him. He chuckled to himself, wondering how much they would be charging for the pay-per-view special: "Baxter vs. Everyone Else."

"So, Doc, can you walk us through it all again?"

"Walk you through what?"

"The death at Saint Augustus the other night."

"Do you mean the one where the guy walked into the emergency room, never said a word, collapsed on the floor, and died right there?

"Do you mean how we tried every possible means of resuscitation, but we were not able to revive him?

"Do you mean how we called his death at 11:59 p.m. on Friday, March 28, 2014?

"Do you mean how the man had no identification, no scars, no identifying marks, and nothing else to indicate who he was or where he came from?

"Do you mean how we have been unable to determine the cause of death, that alcohol and tox screens were negative, and that there were absolutely no other indications as to why his system suddenly shut down? That death?"

"Yes, Doctor, that death."

His sarcasm was lost on that group. "What do you want to know?"

"Can you walk us through it all again?"

"I just did."

"Huh?"

Chris stared blankly at the sheriff. Every conversation he would have from that day on—with the Portland Police Department, the Washington County Sheriff's Office, the Beaverton Police Department, the mayor's office, the medical examiner—would surely be the same.

"No, I never met the guy before..."

"No, he didn't say anything to me..."

"Yes, my father was Sam Baxter. What does that have to do with anything? My dad died over twenty-five years ago...but, of course, you already know that, don't you?"

Chris was tired of doing everyone else's job. He had given them the details on John Doe. He had confirmed with Colleen Fellow from the *Portland Times* the link between John Doe and Sam Baxter. He had even given her the twenty-eighth, sort of. Eventually, someone would have connected both deaths to Friday, March 28. Some conspiracy theorist would have figured out the Friday, March 28 deaths were twenty-eight years apart. That was easy. That was all they would need.

Chris Baxter's Residence

Evening

Chris was finally home for the evening. He was trying to get his head around the interrogation he had just endured—that's exactly what it felt like, an interrogation. He turned on the TV and flipped through the channels. *How am I supposed to know who the hell John Doe was?* As he gazed at the TV, regular programming was interrupted to air the president's unscheduled press conference.

Chris was deep in thought and yet captivated by the voices interrupting his world.

WASHINGTON, DC

White House Briefing Room

"My fellow Americans: I have spent most of the day conferring with leaders from around the world. According to the data supplied by all 195 independent states, there has not been a single confirmed death since approximately 7:00 a.m. on Saturday, March 29, 2014. That's Greenwich Mean Time, so it was 3:00 a.m. here in DC. So far, no one has identified a cause or offered a rational explanation for this event.

"Senior members of the National Institutes of Health and the Centers for Disease Control and Prevention are working closely with the World Health Organization to determine possible medical causes or implications of this extraordinary circumstance we find ourselves in. The vice president is working with Congress and all state leaders to ensure civil order remains intact. The chiefs of staff are continuing to keep the men and women of our armed services at a high level of readiness, both here and overseas.

"At this time, there is no immediate threat to the United States. I'm asking all of our citizens to remain calm and patient as we investigate further. That is all the information I have available. Now, I'll take a few questions."

President Amit Thakar had chosen his words carefully. Even if he had nothing to add, the nation needed to hear from him. The best he could do was stand at the podium and present a convincing rendition of "I don't know what the hell is going on any more than the next guy."

The crowd of reporters erupted in a frenzy of "Mr. President! Mr. President!" After a year in office, they were all familiar faces to President Thakar. He looked around the room for an easy opener.

He pointed. "Kelly."

"Mr. President, do we have an idea if there has been any kind of organized cease-fire or any other efforts to stop violence?" He could always count on Kelly for a softball.

"To our knowledge, no, there has been nothing like that. In fact, initial reports do not show there has been any reduction in violence or crime, in any capacity. The bombing on Sunday outside of our embassy in Kabul severely injured four US soldiers and nine members of the Afghani Consulate. The immediate response from joint medical teams allowed them to save lives, but not without significant trauma.

"Incidents of violence, accidents, natural disasters, and illness have continued, here in our own nation and elsewhere around the world. People are sustaining life-threatening injuries and suffering from critical health issues just as they do every other day of the year—except that since sometime on Saturday morning we haven't had a loss of life..."

The reporters jockeyed into position to get their questions answered. Some wanted to ask a follow-up. Perhaps they could uncover the deeper issue, steer the president to a better focus, or challenge the veracity of his statements. Others waited to ask their question—their perfect question. Thakar knew all the games. He wanted to plug any holes with as much information as he could think of.

"When will we run out of hospital beds?" Kelly interrupted. She knew the rules—this could get her blacklisted from asking questions for a while—but she had to ask this additional question.

"The infrastructure of the United States health care system has a robust capacity for mass trauma, both critical and long care. Since the events of September 11, 2001, we have continued evaluating, improving, and augmenting this system. Until we understand the cause of this anomaly, we can't predict if it is a long-term event or if there are underlying implications. What I can assure you is that we have the facilities and the professionals to provide every citizen the same excellent level of care they were afforded last week." He made a mental note to steer clear of Kelly for a while. He could already envision the backlash from that last comment; it would not go over well in the inner-city, low-income districts he had fought so hard to win in 2012.

"Veronica," he assigned the next question.

“Mr. President, you mentioned 3:00 a.m. Saturday morning here in DC and 7:00 a.m. in Europe. Those times don’t make sense. Seven o’clock Greenwich is midnight on the West Coast.”

“That’s not a question, Veronica. That’s geography.” The crowd chuckled uncomfortably.

“Mr. President, if no one died after midnight, Pacific Time, has anyone considered the fact that this event started on the West Coast? Reports claim there was an unexplained death in Portland, Oregon, last Friday—and that was the last death before this started. What do we know about the situation in Portland? And what about the doctor, Christopher Baxter, who tried to save the man? Do we know anything?”

* * *

As he watched the press conference unfold on television, Chris muttered and cursed, “Goddamn you, Colleen Fellow from the *Portland Times*!”

* * *

The president was quick to respond, “There has been no connection established between any of the events in the last five days and any single person. And for that matter, Veronica, the lack of any confirmed deaths still doesn't mean an event is even occurring at all. I am simply sharing the facts we have now. We are exploring every possibility and every theory. Right now, we can't explain why we haven't had a confirmed death since 3:00 a.m. Eastern Standard Time on Saturday morning. What I will not do is subject a fellow American to inquiry and accusation unjustly."

The president was losing this one as well. He could already read the reaction to "subject a fellow American to inquiry and accusation unjustly." Maybe his chief of staff had been right after all: hold off on speaking to the press until we know more. But he had to do this.

"This is exactly the reason I am holding a press conference now. We cannot let our fear of the unknown drive what we do at this hour. We must remain calm." Reassured by his own words, he took a breath and regrouped.

"Leaders from the City of Portland, as well as federal officials directed by me, have been in contact with Dr. Baxter. Beyond the fact that he specializes in emergency medicine and has firsthand knowledge of events that took place near the beginning of the timeline we are looking at, there is no other connection we know of.

Dr. Baxter is also a retired, decorated Army veteran. For his prior service, and for his continued current support, I can only offer my appreciation."

* * *

Back in Portland, Chris smiled. *I just might vote for him next time.*

* * *

The president's irritation started to show. He pointed again. "Next question. Andrew."

"Mr. President, I've seen reports that fundamentalist Muslim groups in Pakistan, Saudi Arabia, and Iran are using this situation as a calling to rise up against the West. Christian leaders in the Philippines and Ukraine have publicly declared the wrath of God is coming. Are we preparing our military forces for a possible standoff of worldwide religious factions?"

Andy! I could kiss you! was the elated thought running through the president's head as he pulled a piece of paper from his breast pocket. "Nice segue, Andy." More chuckles. "I received two notes early this afternoon. The first was from Iran's supreme leader, Ayatollah Ali Khamenei. Bear with me as I share a paragraph from his pages. He writes, 'There will be a time of great tribulation on earth followed by the appearance of a great Savior who will usher in the Kingdom of God and bring an end to suffering and evil.'

"The note doesn't talk of war or uprising or wrath. Ayatollah Ali Khamenei asked me to view this situation as a sign. I received the second letter just moments after I finished reading the first. It says, 'There will be a time of great tribulation followed by the return of the Messiah, who will usher in the Kingdom of God on earth and bring an end to suffering and evil.'"

No one interrupted or spoke.

"Now, I may be wrong, but I assume that Pope Francis did not co-author his letter with the Ayatollah. Their messages are clear. Whether you believe in the messiah or a savior, whether or not you think there will be a kingdom of God on earth, this is a time of great tribulation. How we respond as Americans, and how we respond as humanity, will determine whether we can bring an end to suffering and evil.

"Thank you, and God bless the United States of America." The president stepped from the podium as the floor erupted.

"Mr. President!"

"Mr. President!"

"Mr. President! Has the Pope been in touch with the leader of Iran?"

"Mr. President! Where is Dr. Baxter now?"

"Mr. President!"

The press conference was over.

The Oval Office

President Thakar hurried back into the Oval Office and slumped onto the couch. He massaged his temples while loosening his tie and collar.

"Well, Mr. President, that went off without a hitch!" His chief of staff refrained from smirking, even as sarcasm flooded the room. Steve Rivers was a man unafraid of speaking his mind with the president. Thakar valued that trait in his inner circle.

"I still think it was the right thing to do, Stephen. I couldn't leave the public in the dark."

Rivers didn't have much time. He asked for a few minutes before the rest of the president's cabinet came in. A few minutes was all he would get. He sat down across from Thakar and assumed the same defeated look.

"Maybe next time you can stick to the canned script, sir. The Republicans are going to have a field day with some of those comments. They are going to gang up against you with this and use it as a weapon in the primaries."

The president conceded, "I know. I know, Stephen. 'Same excellent level of care,' 'inquiry and accusation unjustly.' I could hear their jabs, even as I said the words. How else could I respond to those questions?" Rivers responded to the president with silence.

"Huh? Tell me. As jaded as politics can make you, the straightforward truth has to be the best way to get through times like this." Rivers was never going to convince him otherwise.

"I know, sir. I'm just looking at the big picture."

President Thakar couldn't see any picture that was bigger than the week he was looking at right then. "This is not the time to debate midterms."

With that cue, Steve Rivers rose and opened the door for the rest of the cabinet. Immediately, General Robert Dell, chairman of the Joint Chiefs of Staff, burst through. "Great press conference, Mr. President!"

"Thanks, Rob. How are our forces holding out so far?" The president's team was alone, and he needed their brutally honest advice. He needed to hear from Rob; his subtle message wasn't lost on the general.

"Great, sir. We haven't picked up any warning signals for us to think otherwise." While the two men talked, the rest of the president's cabinet filed in.

More and more bodies piled through the door: so many, in fact, that Department of Housing and Urban Development Secretary Julie Townley, and everyone unfortunate enough to follow her, were relegated to waiting for further instructions out in the corridor. Everyone huddled around the president, prepared to give any information they had.

"All forward-deployed stations," General Dell continued, "have reported in within the last thirty minutes. Two soldiers sustained life-threatening injuries during a firefight in Uganda."

"Why are we there still?" whispered Dr. Vivian Leno, director of the National Institutes of Health, to no one in particular.

"They were sent in as advisers to help find Kony, ma'am," Dell turned and responded to the doctor directly.

Department of Defense Secretary Daniel Mayfield stepped into the conversation before all focus was lost.

“Anything else, General?”

“One Army pilot was injured when his bird had a hard landing in Germany. He’ll be okay. Just some bad cuts and a broken leg. That’s all to report, Mr. President.” General Dell peered over at the NIH director. His message was clear: stay out of my fucking lane, ma’am.

“Thank you, General. Also, the dossier on Colonel Baxter proved to be quite valuable. Your summary is perfect. Thanks.”

“You are welcome, sir.”

The general paused before continuing the conversation. “Sir, I appreciate your confidence in my report. Lieutenant Colonel Baxter is definitely not a threat to us here. He is not associated with the cause of this so-called event.”

Dr. Leno continued to express her skepticism. “Maybe he’s not the cause, but I’m not convinced he’s isn’t a part...”

Dell jumped in immediately: “Baxter served under my command multiple times with SOCOM. We’ve both seen some hairy shit.” Those who didn’t know what his cryptic description referred to only had to take a look at the general's stern face; they shuddered at the possibilities. "A man like Colonel Baxter is not going to jeopardize human lives, or the sovereignty of the United States, intentionally or accidentally. Trust me, he has looked at this situation carefully. If he had seen any connections or links, he would have reached out directly to me."

"Maybe he can't see the link that's there," said Dr. Leno. She would not let it go.

"Doctor, if a pattern or connection exists that he is part of, Baxter would find it. You can't do the things he has done, done for the security of you and your family, and miss anything. There is no connection."

Leno added, "Where did he serve with you?" There was no way Dr. Vivian Leno was going to get an answer. The question was neither responded to nor acknowledged.

"I concur with you, General Dell," said the president. Turning to Secretary Mayfield, he directed, "Mr. Mayfield, please ensure our forces continue their missions per their existing OPLAN. I don't want the fear of being injured or, God forbid, killed, to be the reason for lack of readiness."

"Yes, sir. My men and women know what they volunteered for. They wouldn't have it any other way." The president's confidence in Mayfield's military leadership went a long way toward easing the pain in his temples.

"Thanks, Danny."

The president moved on. "Dr. Hansed, has there been any update on the status of this event?"

"As far as we can tell, the worldwide statistics on injuries and illnesses have not changed in any significant way—neither rise nor decline. It's just..." Health and Human Services Secretary Dr. Laura Hansed paused to form better words, but they weren't there. "It's just that people simply aren't dying."

Rumbling kicked up in the group, just as it did whenever someone uttered that phrase. It's as if every time they heard it, it was the first time—the sheer lunacy of the concept mystified them.

"There's got to be some explanation," injected Vice President Randall Bower.

Dr. Hansed simply shrugged her shoulders and said, "If there is, we haven't found it yet."

It was absolutely absurd. Everyone was in agreement, so there was no sense in raising the point yet again.

The vice president dug further, "What about the question from the press conference? How long before we run out of hospital beds?"

"We have close to a million staffed hospital beds in the United States; more if we set up mobile triage centers. Typically, fifty percent of the beds are in use, so I'd say five hundred thousand beds is a good estimate." She gave them a minute to think about that before diving deeper.

"Let's assume that the US population is still facing death at a rate of about 6,800 per day, only they aren't dying. Instead, they are filling those beds. That's well over two months before we run out of accommodations."

The vice president shook his head in disapproval, even as Dr. Hansed added another murky layer to the health care situation. "I think there are problems that are going to be greater than bed count. Supplies and staff will be taxed, first on the medical side. Social impact is also going to be a problem."

Homeland Security Secretary John Dawson jumped in: "There are two wildcards here. When will people start dying again, and when will society begin to break down from this?" He paused. "Maybe the first question should just be: *will* people ever start dying again? And—and this is the big issue—how will we react?"

Secretary of State Mary Throwe added, "We have no idea what the next step will be. Fourteen nations have declared this as the start of worldwide anarchy. There are at least one hundred confirmed threats from global terror organizations that they will start executing infidels as part of their god's plan, fifteen additional here in the United States. So far, they are only making the threats. No one is following through with anything—yet."

The gathering of cabinet and senior members began to break down. A smattering of thoughts, ideas, and responses flooded the air.

"Maybe they're scared of breaking the streak."

"Maybe they don't want to be first. This way they are justified to retaliate."

"Maybe they don't want to stop a good thing."

"Nobody thinks this is a good thing."

"Maybe everyone's just waiting for the other shoe to drop." Everyone stopped and looked at the Central Intelligence Agency director, Sebastian Key.

"Everything happens for a reason, right? Maybe that reason is that this is actually the great tribulation preceding the end of the world–like the Ayatollah mentioned to you, Mr. President–maybe that reason is simply that we're not able to break this cycle. The truth is, we won't know the reason until we start eliminating variables."

"What are you getting at?" asked President Thakar.

"Sir, I am sure we are not the first group to discuss this behind closed doors. The question is already out there. Can we still die? Every nation is asking the same question. Maybe some already have the answer, and now they're at ease watching the US collapse under the weight of our struggle. Hell, for all we know, some thug in Chicago already knows the truth. Maybe he's walking out of Jackson Park with a grin on his face and our answer on the tip of his bloody knife." Sebastian Key was willing to say what everyone else in the room was thinking.

"Maybe we should see if we can kill someone," Key was comfortable saying the words, but Key was also willing to follow through.

In an instant, Thakar became unglued. He leaped to his feet and confronted Key. "That's never going to happen, Director Key. I am not going to authorize taking a life just to see if it can still happen. Under no circumstances will that be done. Am I clear on that?"

"Yes, sir." Key was direct, unfiltered, and ruthless, but he knew how to take an order.

"The United States will not be the nation that acts in an unjust manner just to see what happens next."

Key left the president with, "Maybe that's the answer everyone else came to as well."

This meeting was going nowhere.

PORTLAND, OREGON

Chris needed to get away. He was now an instant celebrity across the globe. The phone started to ring moments after his name was uttered during the president's briefing. The first was a random coworker who knew his personal cell number, then three more followed in quick succession. He ignored them all. But the last was Milton, a friend he had known since high school, who now lived just a few blocks from him. He picked up and jumped right in. "Milt, I don't think this is going to play out well."

"I'm watching the news right now. What's going on?"

"I don't know, but I need a place to go. I'm about to have every nutjob in Portland try to track me down."

Chris and Milton weren't close friends, but they stayed in contact just enough that there was no need for catch-up or small talk at that moment.

"Are you at home? Get the fuck out of there and come over to my place."

"I'll be there ASAP."

Chris ended the call, turned off his cell phone, and began scrambling around his apartment. For a man desperately trying to run away from the unexpected, his actions were quite efficient, deliberate, and complete. In less than a minute, he managed to grab everything needed: his pack–which he had repacked soon after his return from Mt. Defiance, in anticipation of ad-hoc hikes–his laptop, his "other" phone (old habits die hard), and the 9mm Glock 17 he kept—locked away deep in his closet—just in case.

Bolting through the door, Chris opted to leave his car where it was. It could be of value later, but all it would do now would be to make him an easier target to find. He cut through several yards to get to Milton's back door. His friend was waiting for him. "Come on in, buddy."

"Thank God you reached out, Milt. I'm not sure what my options are right now. Hell, I don't even know what the fuck is going on."

"You're all over the news and the Internet."

CHRIS BAXTER: BACKSTORY

Nothing slowed Chris's pursuit of his career, military precision and excellence, and his dedication to saving lives. In his mind, no one should ever again have to die alone. No one should remain lost and nameless, unclaimed, forgotten.

He thought that everyone should die for a reason. If there wasn't a good reason, then they should be saved. The US Army was the perfect place for Chris to follow through with that belief, and he thrived there.

Until Friday, March 28.

On Friday, March 28, 2008, Major Baxter was attached to the Iraqi Special Operations Forces (ISOF). At that time, he had been in Iraq for nearly two years, as part of a US Army Special Forces team assigned to train the Iraqi people and prepare them for operational handoff while reducing the US military presence in-country. The offensive, *Operation Saulat al-Fursan*, Arabic for "Operation Charge of the Knights," was launched on March 25. When Iraqi troops were overwhelmed by opposition forces of the Mahdi Army militia inside the city, the offensive stalled, requiring American and British air and artillery support. The engagement resulted in a standoff.

There were more than one thousand casualties after six days of heavy fighting.

On March 28, Chris moved from house to house, treating dozens of military and civilian casualties. The Battle of Basra was in some of its heaviest stages.

In the middle of triaging the wounded, Chris looked up as an Iraqi soldier walked through the doorway of the makeshift aid station. Without saying a word, the man collapsed on the floor and died.

Coldly, Chris thought to himself, *I know how he died.* He counted at least eight bullet holes in the soldier's back and neck and a large chunk of metal piercing his side, probably shrapnel from a vehicle explosion. Chris had no time to think about this dead soldier. He had to focus on the men he could save.

Even though he continued to work, Chris was fully aware of the date. He guessed his father had died just like this soldier: with neither warning nor alarm. The memory no longer haunted him, yet he was always aware of it. Had his dad known what was going to happen? Surely, he had to have been scared at some point. What worried Chris was that someday this might happen to him. Would he see it coming? Could he remain calm and collected? Would he be scared?

Chris was indeed aware. Even as his mind revisited those memories and the constant questions they elicited, his energy and focus had to remain on the task at hand: saving troops.

On Friday, March 28, 2008, Chris decided his goal was to return to Portland. Saint Augustus's emergency room was where he could save people from the unknown. He'd get his twenty (he'd be crazy not to) but that was the day a plan was forged to bring Chris Baxter home.

While Chris had stopped fearing March 28th long ago, its randomness continued to mesmerize him.

One final act was needed for Chris to let it go entirely. On Monday, October 22, 2012, Linda Baxter died in her home after a seven-month battle with lung cancer. Chris was relieved. His mom died in her sleep, without having to struggle for another day, another moment of life, as he had seen failing souls do thousands of times before. More importantly, her death had no coincidental connections to anything. October. The twenty second. Monday. Chris knew exactly how she died and where. And the why was clear, too: her two-pack-a-day habit.

After the graveside ceremony a few days later, Linda's neighbor came up to Chris and tried to break the ice. "Do you think that your mom knew she was about to die right in the middle of a solar eclipse?"

"That's the dumbest thing I've ever heard." Chris never gave the solar eclipse a second thought, nor did the twenty eighth ever cross his mind again. His demons were laid to rest forever.

Laid to rest, until Colleen Fellow from the *Portland Times* called him on that Monday morning.

KIDAL, NORTHERN MALI

"It is time."

Zodi Dayak was ready to die. As two women lifted him from the straw mat and held his body steady, one under each arm, a third gently cleansed his gaunt frame with a tattered cloth. In place of his drab garments, Dayak was adorned with a boubou. The full-length tunic splashed a fantastic array of bright yellows, greens, and oranges like bursts of stars streaking across the sky. They gently lowered him onto a litter covered with magnificently embroidered arras, placed a turban on his head—made from the same beautiful cloth as the tapestry—and dressed his feet in leather sandals. Finally, around his neck they placed a copper amulet suspended by a simple leather cord. It was time.

Dayak cherished this rite as his family carried him to the *terrain des adieux* to wait for his turn. His parents had been born free, the first generation never to see slavery in French Sudan. To ensure freedom continued, Dayak took up arms with local rebels in the fight to become an independent nation. After years of rebellion from France and quarrels with its neighbors, the Republic of Mali was formed.

He was still a young man when his goal was completed. His stalwart, muscular frame radiated the will of a nation no longer willing to submit its sovereignty to another.

A small sect of the ordinarily nomadic tribes of northern Mali followed Zodi Dayak upon his victorious return, settling into a village which thrived in this remote region. He never again joined in the varied conflicts that continued in his homeland, choosing instead to remain in his village as their political and spiritual leader. His voice propelled others to follow, and new generations to believe.

But now, as age and sickness consumed his physique, his majestic frame was all but forgotten. But for the faintest of whispers into his daughter's ear, he could no longer form words.

"It is time, my dear."

Zodi Dayak had spent much of his life traversing these farewell grounds. In just the previous year, he had helped to carry three of his grandchildren, unfortunate by-products of ongoing engagements with militants. These grounds held no sadness or grief, for the journey to them was meant to honor the children of the Kidal Region.

He would neither eat nor drink again; Dayak's body rejected any attempt. He would spend the remaining hours of his life in the glorious comfort of the sights and sounds of commemoration.

The people of the region came together to honor their father.

VII - Thursday, April 3, 2014

Five days.

It took the world just under four to recognize that the series of strange events were a global phenomenon. Making sense of them, however, was beyond the grasp of most. Fear of the unknown rarely creates a quest for understanding before a search for blame is undertaken. On the fifth day, Colleen Fellow from the *Portland Times* provided the who, the where, and the when.

But before its fears were corrected or confirmed, the world would demand to know why.

PORTLAND, OREGON

Morning

Chris spent most of the night searching the Internet, reading stories about the miracles and strange events that were taking place all over the world. Portland, and the rest of Oregon, were just like Boston, Mexico City, Madrid, Baghdad, and Tokyo.

At first, every city was a narcissistic adolescent, unable or unwilling to see that their city was no different than others. And when people finally acknowledged that they were merely one part of a global pattern, they all marked an "X" to claim their city, or town, or country, as the outbreak's point of origin. While Colleen Fellow's article in the *Portland Times* echoed every other article in the world, her piece was unique in one important way: rather than bestowing the distinction of the event to the city of Portland, she connected it to one person: Christopher Baxter. One name, and his unique background, went beyond circumstance. The world now had proof this was started by a Baxter, but would it also end because of a Baxter?

As Chris read through the countless reports and the arguments being used to "convict" him in absentia, he was astonished by the overload of information that had already been published:

- Sam Baxter passed this power on to Chris through the Saint Augustus emergency room
- Sam Baxter isn't actually dead.
- Sam Baxter is actually Chris Baxter; he has taken over Chris Baxter's body or is channeling himself through Chris Baxter.
- Chris Baxter was trained by the Army to use his powers.

- Chris Baxter was recruited by the CIA. Chris chuckled when he read this one; it was sort of true, but the kid in China had no way of knowing that.
- Chris Baxter is holding the world ransom.
- Chris Baxter is trying to destroy the world.
- Chris Baxter is the second coming, here to save the world

By early morning, Chris was sure no one could dismiss his culpability in this drama. Hell, the Internet almost had *him* convinced. All anyone needed to ensure Chris's conviction was some sort of crime.

Milton quietly crept out of his bedroom and peered into the study before entering. He walked over to his friend and placed a hand gently on his shoulder. "Hey, buddy. Did you get any sleep?"

"A little bit. I'm trying to figure out what's going on here, Milt."

"Something tells me you're not going to get answers on the www."

Chris stopped looking at the computer, closed his eyes, and leaned back. After debating the possibilities, he sighed deeply and returned to the conversation.

"Yeah, I'm sure you're right, but I just want to know what's feeding this frenzy. It's crazy the stuff that people have dug up to link me to all this shit." Chris turned to the screen. "You know that there's a news station in Denver that has quote/unquote factual accounts about my government recruitment efforts when I was in?"

"Recruiting for what?"

Chris tossed his hands in the air. "My question exactly! They don't say, and apparently they don't have to. Shit, they even have my West Point and med school transcripts posted online. Everything about my life is out there, the facts as well as the ridiculous accusations and innuendoes."

"I know. I read through some of it. I was up reading really late, too. Dude, did you really treat rebels in Thailand?" Chris paused long enough for Milt to walk back the question. "Sorry. None of my business."

"No, Milt. This definitely is your business. Apparently, my house was ransacked about ten minutes after I left last night. There's no saying what would have happened if I had stayed. You took a risk...you are still taking a risk."

"I'm not about to stand by and do nothing while a bunch of random idiots overreact here. They don't even know what's going on. So, what do they do? Boom! They blame you."

"Milt, I'm not sure why you're sticking your neck out like this."

"Because I know you, buddy. You're one of the good guys," Milt affirmed softly.

Suddenly Chris realized Milt really didn't know him at all. Forty-some-odd years of friendship, yet for more than half of it, Chris had squirreled himself away, trying to forget the past. Milton deserved more than having to rely on childhood loyalty.

Chris motioned for him to sit down. "Alright, Milt, no secrets. Ask me what you want to know. Any question. I'll give you the straight scoop, as honestly as I can, based on what I know."

"Anything?"

"Anything at all."

Pulling his chair closer, Milton took a seat. He started with what everyone wanted to know. "What is going on?"

"I have no idea, Milt. That John Doe who died at Saint A's is exactly that to me—a John Doe. I have no idea who he was. I don't even have any idea how he died. I've been racking my brain trying to figure out the answers to those questions. I didn't even make the connection to my dad until that damn reporter called. I was out in the Gorge on Sunday, then buried in medical books Monday and Tuesday, trying to figure out John Doe's case. The cops pulled me in for questioning yesterday morning and...well, you know the rest."

"Have you seen him?"

"Seen who?"

"Sam."

After his initial shock over the sheer lunacy of it, the question didn't seem so crazy to Chris. He reminded himself that most of what his old friend knew about his life today came from the Internet. Chris smiled. "My dad? Milt, my dad's dead. I haven't seen him. He doesn't talk to me. And I am not finishing any work he started."

"Is the stuff I read about you treating rebels in Thailand true?"

Anything at all. Chris took a deep breath. "There's a lot of stuff out there. A lot of it is true, but a lot more of it is bullshit. I was in Thailand at the end of '08. I was attached, as a doctor, to a spec ops team. They were training Yellow Shirts, a political rebel group. I taught their medical teams how to triage casualties." He could see Milton trying to envision it.

"None of our work ever made the newspapers. Few people know we were there, and most of those who were will never admit it. I did a lot of those types of missions while I was in the Army." Chris had seen Milt's expression before. That "holy shit" look.

"How many of those missions did you go on?"

"Nine regions and about thirteen years clandestine total. How does the saying go? 'Win some, lose some'?"

As Milton's comfort with the ground rules grew, so did his curiosity. "Did you see a lot of people get killed?"

Anything at all. "Yes, a lot. I don't know the exact number, but over the years, easily in the thousands. I'm sure of that. People on every side, with various political interests, military, civilians..." Chris paused and swallowed hard, "and lots of kids..."

"How many did you kill?"

"None! I'm a doctor, I don't kill. I was trained to use all of the weapons that our teams carried, and I always carried one of these," he said, patting the Glock strapped to his hip, "but thank God I never had to kill." Looking down, Chris thought about the fear he had carried throughout his army career. “I’m not sure I could even pull the trigger if push came to shove.”

Milton’s curiosity turned more forward-thinking. “What are you going to do?”

“I have no idea. I’m going to bug out right now. I’ll go out past Bend or Hood for a while and keep track of what’s going on from there. There’s not a lot out by Ochoco, and I’ll be out of cell range, which is a good thing. I can get there in about five or six hours.” Patting his backpack, he assured Milton, “I’ve got a satellite phone here that my buddies have kept active, so I can keep up to speed on everything.”

Milton reached into his pocket and tossed Chris his keys. “Who knows what’s happened with your car by now. I bet it’s been searched. And there’s a tracker on it, for sure. Take my SUV. It’ll come in handy in the mountains.”

“Milt, I owe you my life.”

“Whatever, buddy. Get the fuck out of here before rush hour starts up. My car’s always in the garage, so my nosey neighbors won’t miss it.” He pulled out an envelope and handed it to Chris. “Here. It’s $500. Let me know how you are whenever you can. Good luck.”

"Thanks, Milt!"

Milton wrapped his arms around Chris as they embraced for the last time.

"The tank's full, so no need to stop until you're out in the boonies. Two things, buddy. When you get back, I want to hear all of your badass stories." Chris grinned. "And if the world really does go to shit, send some of your army pals to rescue my chubby ass!"

"Done and done," Chris said as he grabbed his things and walked out the door.

"Done and done!"

Chris waited impatiently for the garage to open, unable to look back. He got in the car, throttled the engine, and drove off down the street.

"Done and done!"

SEOUL, SOUTH KOREA

Incheon University Hospital

For two days, Kyle remained by Sarah's bedside, unwilling to leave her for even a moment and unable to face the shame he felt was waiting for him outside. He leaned over the bed and with the gentlest of touches, kissed his daughter's forehead. "Happy birthday, sweetie."

Song Bung-ju appeared in the doorway, a beautiful display of mugunghwa in his hand. "We had a special day prepared for Ji-hyun today." The flowers were in full bloom, splashing infinite blends of pink and magenta. Bung-ju spoke English remarkably well. His mother, Mary's sister, wanted her son to have the advantages that fluency in English afforded.

Kyle was grateful and humbled by the kindness of this man who, even though he was family, was someone he didn't know at all. "I know Sarah wanted to visit Korea more than anything else in the world. Thank you for all you've done for her."

"What have the doctors said, Mr. Kyle?"

When Kyle looked at Bung-ju, he no longer saw a stranger. He saw something familiar in his eyes, a look Sarah had whenever she was somber. He saw the same melancholy expression Sarah's grandfather had when Mary told him she and Kyle were going to be moving to the United States. He saw family. Kyle reached out for his nephew's hand. "Bung-ju, please. I am family. I am your ee-moh-noo," his mother's brother-in-law. "Please call me that or just Uncle."

"Okay, Uncle. I prefer that. None of my other friends have an 'uncle.' They all will be so jealous when I get to introduce you!" Kyle shuddered at the thought of returning to Wonju. Eighteen years had passed since he left, since he had buried his wife on a hillside close to her childhood home. "I don't think I am welcome there anymore. I took Mi-rim away from her family. I brought her back here and she died. Then I left with our infant daughter." Kyle looked longingly at Sarah. She looked just like her mother. "And now, I bring that child back only to die as well. It's the same." The bandages covering her face and body exposed only traces of the girl he remembered.

* * *

Bung-ju had witnessed the entire tragic event. He had been waiting for Sarah at the airport, watching every plane as it landed, watching for the one that carried his cousin. He looked on in disbelief as a plane screeched down the runway in a fantastic explosion of sparks and flames, and he heard the crushing boom that followed. All he could think of was how long it took for the sound to hit him after the sky lit up. Then he thought of Ji-hyun.

Over six hours would pass before Bung-ju would find where the medics had taken her. During the ensuing chaos, no one had time for him. To them, he was just a random kid. More than once, he was shoved aside by groups of grieving family members who were also searching for information, and by frantic airport officials who were rushing here and there. After someone from the airline took down his name, the passenger's name, and a description of what he saw, he was dismissed. Updates were only being released to family members—long-lost cousins didn't qualify.

The airport became a segregated holding pen. In one section, inconvenienced travelers fought to reschedule their flights. Bung-ju stayed with the other group. He waited for updates. When he was able to make a connection on the saturated cell phone lines, he called his family in Wonju to share what he knew. The group stayed together. Occasionally it would reduce in size when a passenger from the ill-fated flight was located, or when someone left in frustration.

Bung-ju jumped when someone screamed in his ear, "Song Bung-ju! Song Bung-ju!" The driver was standing about three feet away from him, unaware that his fare was so close. Sent by Kyle, the driver had been hired to take him to Sarah and to help him in whatever way he needed.

* * *

When Kyle arrived at the hospital, he found Bung-ju in the waiting room, pacing back and forth while Sarah was undergoing yet another operation. "No, Uncle. Ji-hyun will not die. We still have too much to do and see. I am going to show her all of Korea. I want to share all of our wonderful food. She is going to take me to the United States to visit Atlanta. I told her that I will not be able to travel for some time because I am starting in the army in a month. I think I will do just the minimum time that I must. After that, I want to come visit you both."

It pained Kyle to hear his nephew talk like that...to have so much faith. Bung-ju was so excited to finally have a cousin, an American cousin. Kyle knew what it was like to suddenly have your whole world shut down, especially when it was a world much grander than the one you hoped to leave behind.

"Sarah says that I need to have an American name when I come to Atlanta. She said that people look at her funny when she says her name is Ji-hyun. What do you think, Uncle? I was thinking Billy would be good."

Kyle smiled. "Billy is nice, but"—his smile disappeared—"Sarah won't be going home. She has major damage throughout her body. They've had to remove more of her left leg, all the way up past here," he leveled his hand across his hip. "Her lungs keep filling with blood and they're not sure her heart can hold out much longer. Her body is too weak. Any more surgery will probably kill her. If she ever wakes up, all she will know is pain."

He suddenly wondered if his daughter could hear him. If she could, Kyle wanted to guide Sarah one more time. "It would be better if she just died."

"No, Uncle. That won't happen. I read on the Internet that people don't die anymore. Ji-hyun will get better."

The odd statement meant nothing to Kyle. Ignoring it, he gazed down at his daughter's lifeless body and prayed for the next step.

How did it get to this? he wondered. *Everything I've worked for, everything I've done to improve life for my family, and here I am again. Sitting in a hospital in Korea watching the love of my life die...again. This time, though, I am praying that she will die.*

The hospital blended modern technology with traditional Korean values. Sarah's ward was equipped with everything needed for an extended visit. Her large room was designed to comfort family members while the staff cared for the patients. Kyle's assistant had hired a small army of people to tend to him and Bung-ju. He had arranged to have cots brought up, communicated with Kyle's extended Korean family, and hired staff to feed the two men. There was nothing for them to do but be with Sarah.

Bung-ju sat and prayed that his cousin would take the time she needed to get better.

Kyle sat and prayed for his daughter to take the time she needed to die peacefully.

OREGON

Ochoco National Forest

Late Afternoon

As Chris struggled to comprehend his supposed role in the event, he got a close-up look at the chaos to which humanity had succumbed. During his seven-and-a-half-hour drive out of Portland on Highway 26, the world's population seemed split into two factions. The "world-is-saved" zealots gloriously embraced a variety of religious beliefs, scientific marvels, and political ideologies that had them convinced that humankind had finally figured out how to live as one with nature and with each other. Those proclaiming "The world is doomed" held to the same tenets, only they interpreted them as the beginning of the end...

Radio stations, at least the ones that were still transmitting live and not playing pre-recorded prayer music, chronicled the hysteria. Thirty-five minutes after the stock market opened, trading was halted—the Dow had already dropped by over fifty-five percent. Families huddled together. Most international air travel was suspended; countries began to close their borders even as masses were flooding to holy centers around the world: the Vatican, Mecca, Varanasi, Jerusalem, the temples in Tibet. In the United States, many mosques, temples, and churches offered both repentance and salvation. Hedonists indulged themselves with an overabundance of the flesh, the bottle, and the needle.

Regardless of how they translated the event, all were assured an unparalleled experience.

Portland, Oregon, of all places, was now widely considered the likely source of this pandemic. Chris's apartment, ransacked overnight, and now considered a shrine of sorts, was being visited by people who wanted to offer thanks or ask for forgiveness. There were reports of jammed traffic and spectators filling every possible space for blocks around his house. Chris knew he had left just in time. He thanked Milt once more as he continued to drive.

Bumper to bumper.

Stop and go.

Wide open.

As Chris drove, he continued to think about John Doe and his father. *What do the two men have in common besides the exceptional similarities surrounding their deaths?* As far as he could tell, there was no other obvious link. "Just me," he corrected himself as he drove by a broken-down station wagon. Three kids were playing over a dirt berm while a man, presumably their father, studied the engine. Chris wondered where they were going. *Where is mom? The car is packed pretty tight. Were they planning on returning home someday? The bicycles on the roof rack make sense, but why did they bother to pack a floor lamp?* He knew there must be some connection. He agreed with Colleen Fellow, and all of the conspiracy theorists: there must be something. But what?

"Ah, hell! There's still time. It's only been six days."

These thoughts occupied Christopher Baxter's mind for 214 miles.

Just a bit before reaching the trailhead, he pulled into a rest stop in Prineville, hoping no one would recognize him with his shaggy mop and scruffy face.

A weary-looking attendant, probably no more than nineteen years old, lumbered his way over to Chris. "Fill 'er up?" he asked before he walked back to unscrew the gas cap.

"Please. Unleaded." There were a few other people in the station, but no one seemed to recognize or pay any attention to Chris. As he watched the travelers, he longed to ask each one about their version of what was going on. Where were they going? Why? Were they running to something or someone, or running away?

"Cash up front, mister." The demand broke Chris out of his thoughts. "Sorry, but it's a pretty crazy day. The card readers are down, and a few people have already tried to bolt without paying." Chris looked over at the pump. On top of it was a cardboard box, covered with magic marker scribbling, with a flap cut out and taped down to the front.

The makeshift sign over the meter read, "$10/gallon." Chris had seen this kind of price-gouging many times before, in Bosnia, Thailand, Angola. He knew that if there was a crisis and a need, there was always a solution, but it would cost you. He dug into his pocket for the money Milton had given him. "Here you go. I shouldn't need more than twenty-five gallons." Chris handed him a folded wad of bills and continued his people-watching. It only took a few minutes before the kid tapped on his roof, eager to get the next car in and drain the rest of the gas from the tanks.

Chris realized he hadn't eaten anything for over a day and knew it might be a while before he got a nice hot meal, so, with a full tank, he headed to the diner at the other end of the rest stop.

The patrons looked like the people he had seen at the gas station and on the side of the highway. Everyone was wrapped up in their own lives, ignoring everything else around them. The waitresses looked like the kid at the gas pump, shuffling along, waiting to run out of food. He wondered, *Did they have nowhere to go, no one to go to? Or, were they exactly where God wanted them?*

After ordering a burger and fries with the fewest words possible, Chris sat at the counter and watched the news on TV. Every time the same recycled photographs were shown, Chris was struck by how young he looked. Just as he thought, no one would be able to identify him based on those photos. With the limited information available, the news kept repeating the same stories, but he couldn't stop watching. Plus, he wasn't ready to drop off the grid just yet. He ordered another soda, then a burger to go, then a double fudge sundae and a cup of coffee. No one spoke to him; travelers, even those by themselves, were not interested in small talk with a stranger. Chris sat alone, quite content, until finally his urge to leave became a priority. He paid the $120 price-gouging bill and bought a few bags of jerky sticks and the last three gallons of water before hopping back into Milton's CR-V.

Christopher J. Baxter was ready to fade away.

After a long day of driving and hiking, Chris was relieved to settle in near the Twin Pillars. April frost made that an ideal place for him to avoid society. The wilderness area blended rugged terrain carpeted with luscious green moss, towering pines, and snow brush. As he walked, nature's springtime bloom soon turned emerald, then faded to brown; deadfall replaced mossy evergreens. The pair of two-hundred-foot volcanic spires dominated the backdrop. Peeling off the trail after about five miles, Chris ventured into the high desert terrain in search of an ideal spot to camp. He settled in among a dense pack of sagebrush. Minimal preparation was needed for the site, and with no expectation of rain, Chris's main concern was the freezing temperature during the night. Burrowing a path into a thick brush offered him additional protection from any curious wildlife, a healthy supplement to his odorous markings outlining the perimeter.

All settled in, Chris unpacked his laptop and satellite phone. The thing looked more like an oversized, outdated cell phone than a high-tech tactical device, but it allowed him to search online way out in that remote sanctuary.

He was fully aware that the moment he powered on the unit and the green phosphorous screen showed a connection, his location would be tracked by various organizations. "If things really do get bad enough," Chris mumbled to himself, "I am going to need them." There was no need to think about the other possibility: if he ended up becoming one of their targets, they'd find him anyway. "At least I get to surf the 'net a little before they come." With a subtle smirk of amusement, he hit the red power button. The clunky screen momentarily displayed SEARCHING before showing a solid connection and full battery charge. READY.

Chris laid a towel on the ground, then pulled his pistol from its holster. As he ran his hands across its rough surface and around the grip, contoured to fit each finger, he wondered if he would be able to use it to kill, if necessary, or if he would remain the man Milton knew. Chris turned his attention to fieldstripping and cleaning his Glock.

Four minutes passed before the call came in. Across the screen were the words SAD-FORAGE. Despite the random call sign, Chris answered immediately.

"What's the matter, Scotty, was SAD-SACK taken?"

"Bax, I'm just happy to hear that you're still SAD."

Abbott and Costello were still in rare form. On each end of the call, though, the old friends choked up a bit, relieved to hear each other's voices again.

Gipson threw the next jab. "What the fuck are you doing out there? Did you get bored in retirement? Tired of handing out tampons to the country folk?"

Chris Baxter and Scott Gipson had been classmates at West Point, and roommates throughout their plebe year. The boy from Portland, Oregon and the boy from Portland, Maine were a constant source of entertainment for the upper-class cadets. Chris often tried to explain that he was actually from Beaverton, Oregon, but that only made matters worse.

"Who are you showboating for these days?" Chris knew he didn't have the security clearance for Colonel Gipson to answer his question, and anyway, he didn't need to know–it was just idle chatter.

"Whatever, Bax. I just can't wait to get out of this shithole. If you had done the job right the first time, I wouldn't be back mopping up your mess." Wherever Scott was right then, the two of them had been there together in the past. That narrowed down Scott's whereabouts to five locations.

Gipson picked up his Glock, freshly cleaned and reassembled. He raised the pistol and lined its sights, aiming at nothing in particular, before taking a deep breath.

"Chris," Scott's tone turned serious, "what's going on back there? Your name is plastered all over this mess."

"I don't know." Baxter picked up his Glock, freshly cleaned and reassembled, as he told his friend everything he had told the reporter, Colleen Fellow, explained to Sheriff Coleman and his posse, and confessed to Milton. He didn't need to tell Scott about the haunting of March 28th. He didn't need to fill him in on his father either; Scott already knew about both. In fact, he probably knew as much about Sam as Chris did. Chris felt no need to convince Scott of anything. This was his long-time friend with whom he had been through so many trials; he felt nothing but unconditional support. Scott just wanted to talk to him and see if and how he was keeping it all together. There were some things they both needed to say, and hear, out loud.

"You can't run," said Scott. "You know that, right?"

"I know."

"If you run, you're guilty. Even if there's no crime, you'll be tried and convicted before they find you."

"I know. I just needed to get away for a few days to figure this shit out. Maybe we can see how it all unfolds."

"They're not looking for you." Chris knew that meant the US Army, the CIA, or the SAD. "They have their hands full right now. Nobody's dying, which means that every analyst is focused on trying to calculate when the shit's gonna hit the fan and lots of bodies start piling up."

"My guess is Saturday," Chris uttered with an almost indifferent tone. Scott didn't respond to the quip.

"Everyone on our side wants to be ready when this hits so that we're not the ones who pull the short straw. Once this breaks, they're going to free up resources. They're going to want to talk to you, Bax. Get to them first, before you're a target."

"I'm not sure where I'll be welcome right now."

"Get up to Lewis. Sim's got the Group up there."

"Phil-freakin-Simchi is in command of First Group? That fucker couldn't find his own ass with a map and compass!" The levity lightened their conversation, but both men knew Colonel Simchi was top notch and a born leader.

"Yeah. Go figure. I'll give him a sit-rep on you."

"Sounds good, Colonel." Chris popped to attention, held the phone out with his left hand and snapped it a sharp salute.

"Listen, Bax. Don't fuck around on this one. I checked the log just now. No one is tracking your sat phone except me, but that will change. Turn it off and leave it off till you get to JBLM. When you get there, call me, or go straight to Sim. Get there by 1800 tomorrow and plan on linking up at the Palm. Do you remember where that is?"

Baxter understood playtime was over.

"I remember."

"Do you have food, fuel, cash?"

"I'm stocked."

"Of course, you are. Don't blow this off, Chris. There's a ton of shit going on, and people are scared. Don't expect the reactions you would usually rely on. Don't trust anyone."

Chris focused on the change in Scott's voice. Devoid of humor, Chris had seen this scene play out hundreds of times before, only now he was the victim. He was now the oppressed soul in a strange land. Colonel Scott Gipson was now there to save him. Chris just hoped he would do the job right the first time.

"WILCO."

"Good luck, Bax. Hold fast tonight and move out tomorrow morning before one. The sun will come up after you're past Portland."

"Scotty, I owe you my life for this." Chris felt like he was starting to owe his life to a lot of people.

"Go to bed, Baxter. It seems like I'm still wiping your goddamn nose."

"Beat Navy, Scotty!"

"Beat 'em!"

The call dropped. Chris powered off the phone and stuck it back in his pack. He looked out toward the horizon, searching for any sign of life. There was nothing. For as far as he could see, in every direction, nothing moved. Even the wind abandoned him as darkness replaced life.

There was no moon that evening. Zero percent illumination.

Chris Baxter was all alone.

For the second time in the day, his mind filled with a somber thought—a friend he would never laugh with again.

VIII - Friday, April 4, 2014

KIDAL, NORTHERN MALI

Celebrations were underway honoring Zodi Dayak's life and legend. By Western standards, he was an old man. In this region of the Sahara Desert, eighty-three years was the kind of longevity reserved for gods. If not for the anesthetizing properties of the kola nuts he chewed, he would have wept all the time. Now, he had little to offer the children he once nurtured. In fact, he was now a strain on them.

Vulnerable to infections that were ravaging his body, blind, mute, and with once-strong limbs now hanging heavy and limp by his side, Zodi Dayak wanted to die. This was not selfish; he was thinking of his family. He embraced the village's need for another elder to replace him.

His clan soothed him in his final days with traditional Malian music and dance. For the remaining bit of his life, Zodi Dayak would sit in the *terrain des adieux*, gently swaying his head to the rhythm of the drums and stomping of the dancers.

There was nothing more to do...

HUMANITY'S RESPONSE

An uneasy peace set in as people began to see the world in the light of the new reality.

Throughout history, many had longed for another chance to live, for both themselves and for those they cherished, yet most ultimately accepted death as a fact of nature. By Friday, April 4, however, the world began to realize "natural" was a term worthy of reconsideration.

Strange occurrences and incredible feats of resilience continued to occupy center stage in the global news. It was a time of praising the gods who let it happen and expressing thanks for the pause in the hatred so many felt for each other. But thanks and praise, when they stay past their welcome, are fickle allies. Some prayed for mercy, some prayed to find a cure, some prayed to stop the demon responsible for *it*. Everyone was gripped by fear. Fear of the wrath God was preparing to unleash. Fear that someone, or some country, was to blame. Military forces everywhere were concerned with when and where the culprit would play its next card, and how to best prepare for it. Fear of what started *it* in the first place.

Would anyone find a cause? Would anyone find a cure? When, if ever, would this curse run its course?

Ochoco National Forest

Morning

Chris never had any intention of following Scott's suggestion to go to Joint Base Lewis-McChord, linking up with Simchi, or confronting any other part of the US Army.

The previous night, he had luxuriated under the protection of the Twin Pillars. Falling asleep soon after darkness fell—he knew that uninterrupted, peaceful slumber was the best remedy for his aching heart and a pounding head—Chris slept for more than ten hours. The slow rise and fall of his chest wasn't enough to split the frosted dew that glazed his sleeping bag. Only when the alarm gently hummed at 7:00 a.m. was there proof of life underneath the sheen of ice.

With a full agenda set for the day, Chris stretched to fight off the last bit of hibernation. He crawled out of his sleeping bag, out of his hide site within the brush, and into the early morning glory that welcomed him. The motions were such a familiar ritual. In less than ten minutes, he was alert, relieved, dressed in fresh clothing, and fully repacked except for his morning kit. He set the grill-top coffee maker on the fire and opened two packs of beef jerky. When the coffee was ready, he poured himself a piping hot cup.

Chris gazed in wonderment at the Herculean sunrise pulling fresh light across the sky. No other daybreak in the world—neither the Noshaq peaks of Afghanistan nor the rocky beachfront range north of Chonglin, far up the North Korean peninsula, could compare to the sunrises in Oregon. Chris didn't want the sun to finish rising, for he wasn't sure what would happen next.

"I'll miss this most of all," fell from his lips before he had a chance to dismiss the misgiving.

When the sky was drained of night and the pot drained of coffee, Chris packed the rest of his things. His satellite phone and 9mm pistol were secured firmly on the outside of his pack, readily accessible should he need them. Once the site was restored to its pre-intrusion condition, he hiked toward the trailhead. It didn't take him long to reach the vehicle.

Chris headed down Highway 26 on his way home one final time. Everything looked the same as the day before. People were milling about aimlessly, as if they had no agenda or destination. Cars, trucks, and SUVs were stuffed with loved ones and personal items deemed essential for the end of the world. Some were able to drive past the growing number of accidents and breakdowns, but more joined the ranks of the useless vehicles, proving the end of mortality did not extend to machinery. Some waited at gas stations and rest stops for some kind of news or guidance, but none was forthcoming.

Chris took notice of one oddity. Even though traffic was heavy and vehicles were piled up by the side of the road, his own journey was unhindered. There was always a gap for him to pass through, an open space that would seal itself off again once he escaped. He would reach his destination in time. The conditions made it so.

HELMAND PROVINCE, AFGHANISTAN

Late Afternoon

Stopping just outside the town of Marjah, close to the triangle that fixes Iran, Afghanistan, and Pakistan, Captain Torim got out of his Humvee and looked around. Intelligence reports had flagged the town, where cross-border leaders of separate Taliban sects regularly met, as "transitioning"—a term that had not yet been defined—but Torim was convinced he and his company would soon find out. Impending turmoil in this region threatened to interrupt the week's strange and unexpected lull.

So far, the joint efforts of the Pakistani and Iranian governments to tighten the noose around the Taliban in Marjah had been successful. Local Afghani informants had provided information that Taliban leaders were planning to meet with a newly unified group known as the Islamic State of Iraq and the Levant or ISIL. The meeting, they said, was supposed to take place somewhere in Marjah, sometime in the next few days.

The order for Captain Torim's company was to find where and when.

Based on critical intelligence, their plan was to use surgical airstrikes to kill key leaders from all three Taliban nations, as well as leaders of ISIL, although no one yet knew who those leaders were. They were going to use long-range surveillance techniques to spot any movement into Marjah. Those entering the area would be digitally tagged by drones and tracked by marines on the ground until it could be determined whether they were part of the planned meeting.

While this was a clearly defined mission, Torim wished his command would address some of its high-risk components. When the order was first issued on Wednesday, he had tried to reason with his commander. "Sir, Marjah is over one hundred square miles with ninety-thousand some-odd locals. How does intel expect us to monitor all traffic in and out? Over."

"*Just in,* Captain. Don't worry about outbound during this operation. Our eyes in the sky will help find traffic. You and your teams just track and identify in. Over." Captain Torim knew the land; this was his fourth tour in Afghanistan, his third in Helmand. While other marines were struggling to find what was out there, he already knew what was coming.

"We're getting into poppy harvest season here, sir. This place is already starting to fill up with every opium producer in the region. Mules aren't far behind. That's a lot of traffic in, over." Torim released the button on his handset and wondered how the hell they were going to fix the mess. He was reasonably sure the US military would not stand his marines directly in front of a tidal wave of violence.

"I'm sending you another company-plus to augment your numbers. You're in command of this task force. Congratulations, Captain. One-six actual, out." Before he was able to continue trying to reason with his commander, the line went dead. Torim walked over to his command tent, dropped the receiver inside and issued the first warning order to prepare for mission expansion.

Now in command of an augmented task force, Torim reflected on a conversation he had had a few days earlier with his driver, a pimple-faced lance corporal, no more than eighteen years old. While in the process of monitoring twenty separate patrols active across Marjah, as Torim stepped back in the vehicle, he had quipped to his driver, "I guess this is one way to fast-track our next promotion." The lance corporal smiled, happy to see his commander finally lightening up; Benji Torim finished the sentence but kept it to himself: *but if bullets ever do start flying again, we're all going to die in this fucking sand.* Instead, he focused on the mission. "Let's move out to our next observation point, Johnny."

"Yes, sir."

PORTLAND, OREGON

Saint Peter's Episcopal Church

Afternoon

Chris quietly strolled the grounds of Saint Peter's. Two years ago, shortly after his mother had died, in an attempt to find peace in the world without her, he had returned to church for the first time in many years. Although his dad's death no longer constantly occupied his thoughts, he was dismayed that his connection to his mom's last day never filled the vacuum. He needed to look ahead and celebrate the future. By holding on to dark memories of the past, his life was devoid of elation. Both in and out of the Army, he was surrounded by death and loss. His job was always to fight to limit loss, to delay death. He needed to find a community. So he had tried going to church. He figured, why the hell not?

When he was a kid, Chris attended Catholic Sunday service every week by himself. When he went, it was a win-win situation for him and his mother. Chris got time at church—a chance to grow spiritually and emotionally—and Linda got two hours to herself, usually spent doing laundry or preparing Sunday dinner. Each week, his mom would hand him a donation envelope, kiss him on the cheek, and send him off.

When Chris graduated high school, he left the church. Nothing specific happened—he just stopped going without giving it so much as a second thought. But after his mother died, he found the need to explore religion again, convinced there had to be more to it than the rituals he engaged in as a child. It was no surprise that Saint Peter's was the church he chose when he began his new phase. The sprawling grounds were perfect for walking, to unwind from life in the hospital, and to avoid contact with others. Talking just to talk never suited him.

On this Friday, Chris walked down the paved asphalt walkway. Just as the path turned to packed dirt, just before he was enveloped by towering evergreens and western red cedars, he heard a voice behind him. Sue rushed to catch Chris before he faded from sight. "I thought it was you out here, Chris."

"Oh, hi there, Mother Sue." Chris feigned surprise rather poorly; he had hoped for a chance to chat with the rector.

Reverend Susan Taple preferred to go by just Sue, or Susan, but after eighteen years in the Catholic Church and twenty-four years in the military, Chris knew firsthand what it took to earn a title and thought it was important to use them correctly.

"It's been a few weeks since you've joined us. We miss seeing you at mass. I know you've been going through a difficult time."

"Weekend rounds at the hospital. Sorry."

That wasn't what Sue meant. "It seems you've become a bit of a celebrity around here." She slowed her pace to match Chris's.

They walked in silence for more than five minutes before he opened up.

"You already know how I've spent my life battling random circumstances. The fact that so many important events in my life had to be more than just random was something I always focused on, clung to." Sue walked with him and listened. "I invented patterns and cycles out of disconnected events."

Cobblestones replaced dirt, changing the landscape once again. "March 28th was my invention. Remembering what happened on that date, trying to give the date a place in my future, was something I was burdened with for years. Because of that day, every year I made decisions that would affect the other 364." The fact that leap years interfered with his math was not overlooked by either of them—Chris and Sue both chuckled silently. Chris ran his hand along the leaves of the undergrowth. "After all those years, when my mom died, I finally put that all aside. Random is just that: random. 'There's no connection—"

"Unless you make a connection. And then the bond is only there for as long as you hold on to it.' That's what you yourself said,

Chris. Remember, this isn't our first walk out here talking about this very same topic. I think we spent three hours on it the first time."

"Yeah. And on many walks after."

Time on the meandering trail with Sue was a good way for him to focus on his own serenity. "I truly let it go, but it is always great to share the freedom I feel from doing so!"

"Chris, you did not let it go. You just turned and shifted its focus. 'March 28th' turned in to 'March 28th doesn't matter.'" He didn't like where the conversation was going. "But, you know, it's okay. Your obsession was redirected into something positive. Your family here loves you, and we love having you celebrate with us when you come. Your time with the hospital, your community work, the church, these are all great outlets. Whatever demons followed you for so many years are now gone." Sue stopped and looked at Chris. "Are you revisiting those random dates right now, Chris?"

Chris smiled. "Nope. And when I leave these grounds, I don't replay a moment. The next time I think about any of this will be when I come back and walk with you. I'm not spiritually cheating on you, Mother Susan!" With his hands together, the way he was taught to pray as a child, Chris topped his affirmation with a lighthearted "I promise."

Sue smiled and began walking again.

"For the past two years, I even forgot it was the date of my dad's death and only remembered after the fact." Chris stopped at looked at Mother Sue. "But what's happening now is different. I have reporters dredging up my past, trying to find a link. I have police telling me they want to know my connection to last week's John Doe." As he reflected on his experience, his voice became turbulent. "Apparently, I'm a global icon, and all because the last man to die in the world did so on my watch. Even now, I can't say that without astonishment at the absolute absurdity of it."

"I know. Michael is bragging about you at school. You've become an overnight legend." Chris smiled; he was still not completely used to female priests with families and children—so different from his Catholic childhood.

"But what's all of this about? How can the entire country, the entire world, think that I have something to do with any of this?"

"Not everyone thinks that."

Out of desperation, Chris lunged at her for salvation. "You're the holy one here. Tell me. Why would God do this to me?"

"God would never do this to you."

"Then what? Is this the rapture or end of times we were told about in Sunday school? I always pictured Judgment Day more like a zombie apocalypse, when the dead all come back to life and walk the earth. I never thought people would just stop going away."

The walk was nearly complete, as the pathway broke out of the trees and pavement resumed under their feet. Sue stopped and grabbed Chris by both hands. She pulled him closer and lowered her head in prayer. "Something will change. It has to."

"Why is all of this happening?"

Sue didn't answer right away. It suddenly occurred to Chris that the past week had also been rough for her, not only because she had a lot of frightened parishioners to soothe, but that this had probably had a significant impact on her own faith. Did she see this as a sign that the end was near? He anxiously awaited her words, for assurance—for faith.

"Sometimes things are just random and don't have a connection." Chris heard his own words turned back towards himself.

"Touché, Sue. Touché." There was nothing more to say.

PORTLAND, OREGON

Colleen Fellow quickly reaped the benefits of her exposé. She was recognized as the reporter who broke the story. UPI called—that was her dream—to find out if she had any more information to offer. Her boss at the *Portland Times* wanted her to conduct a follow-up interview with Baxter before the police got to him. She felt as if she had finally made it to the big time.

After scouring the newspaper's archives for information that might help her figure out where Baxter had gone, Colleen called more than fifty people, both known or potential contacts of his, including Milton. But no one had seen Chris; no one knew where he was; everyone told her about how she had ruined Chris's his life by involving him in the crisis. She dismissed the comments. "Hey, I'm just doing my job."

Gradually, Colleen got an idea of the man Christopher Baxter truly was. She heard tale after tale of a shy little kid torn to pieces by the trauma his father had endured. Tales of the many lives Dr. Baxter had saved, both in the Army and as a civilian, starkly contrasted with the kind of person who would conceive the event the world was currently facing.

Colleen discovered the level of diligence and integrity she would need to find if she would ever succeed as a journalist—she would never wholly cleanse the stain of those lessons.

BEAVERTON, OREGON

Chris rifled through his backpack for a clean pair of socks. With fresh feet, he grabbed his Glock, just in case, tossed the rest of the gear in the backseat, and abandoned Milton's SUV in the parking lot of Saint Peter's.

He wanted to look at every site that had lured him back to Oregon three years earlier. After giving a wide berth to his nearby apartment, Chris walked for the rest of the day. On April 4 everything was different, yet nothing had changed, even after so many years.

After leaving Saint Peter's, Chris trekked seven or eight miles back to Beaverton to take a stroll past the place where his childhood home used to be, even though the original building was no longer there. His mother had been the last holdout on her block. When she passed, and Chris sold the property, developers immediately leveled the house to begin construction on new townhomes. He thought it was all for the best. While he'd had no desire to move back in with all those memories, he cringed at the thought of another boy living and growing up there.

Standing before the location, Chris could see the tiny, one-level ranch just as it had been back in '98. Before going off on the next adventure, he had a few weeks of leave. Chris had decided to repaint the outside to Linda's favorite color—god-awful lime green became god-awful powder blue.

"Mom, you did have a flair for the bold!"

Though the entire block was now different, it didn't take much for Chris to envision the choppy asphalt street where he'd learned to ride a bike. Just beyond their driveway was his favorite hiding spot when playing hide-and-go-seek with Milt and the gang. He could still see the dilapidated steel shed he had been hiding behind when Linda had come out to tell him Sam was dead. No, the thought of another boy inheriting those memories would never do.

Chris wanted to stop and pick up some roses before visiting his mother in the cemetery. Because of his celebrity status, he chose to avoid people, at least until he was ready for this to end. When he neared her gravesite, he was surprised to see flowers surrounding the headstone. Apparently, being Chris Baxter's mother came with certain perks. He picked up one of the white roses lying across her grave and paused for a moment before gently placing it atop his mother's headstone. For the next five minutes, he stood in peaceful silence. No thoughts, worries, or anguish passed through his mind. He kneeled to kiss the words "LINDA BAXTER" that were etched across the marble slab.

Sam Baxter had never earned a cemetery plot. His body had been cremated after the investigations were completed in 1986, but his ashes had never been returned to his family. On the day his mother had been laid to rest, Chris had etched a slot near the base of a magnificent white oak providing shade and protection to Linda's final home. Into it, he had wedged his father's police shield. He gently traced his hands across the bark until he found the scar that covered the badge he'd hid. Next to his father's legacy, he dug a second notch and forced in one of his own dog tags—a remnant of his army days, no longer needed. Chris was warmed by the fact that he and his father would grow together and continue to provide the overwatch his mother deserved.

Chris left the cemetery and traveled to his final destination: Saint Augustus.

PORTLAND, OREGON

Almost Midnight

Chris gazed across the parking lot of Saint Augustus Hospital, thinking about the week's events and how they connected to his past. There was so much he would never know or uncover, yet he refused to stop trying.

Before taking another step, he confronted his fears out loud. "Which memories are real, Chris, and which ones are imagined—merely moments created in your mind? Is there ever a point where these two converge? If there is, is there a barrier between them or do they blend into a new truth? Why would this happen in my world? What a preposterous discussion!" It only served to heighten his anxiety.

Knowing he had answers to the questions everyone had been wrestling with all week made him feel slightly better.

When is the event going to end? Will it ever?

“Yes,” Chris whispered softly. “Yes, it will.”

A week without death had a strange impact on the hospital. Usually, at this late hour, there were only a few cars parked in the lots—those belonging to the staff inside working the overnight shift. That night, the lots were full. Patients who normally would transition from this life to death were refusing to let go. No one knew what to do. Family members, unsure what their loved ones needed, refused to leave their bedsides. Zealots of all viewpoints came to protest, pray, repent, or condemn. Some stood with cameras and pens at the ready, simply to see what would happen next and to be there when it did. Every arrival to the now-infamous Saint Augustus emergency room sparked a media frenzy.

Chris was relieved to return, glad to just be there, even if he would never again have the opportunity to practice his profession again. Even though everyone knew him at Saint Augustus, he checked to make sure he had his identification. Yes, his wallet was there, in his pocket, just below the holstered pistol on his hip.

As he started to walk slowly toward the main doors of the emergency room, Chris wondered just how close he would be able to get before someone recognized him. How would his colleagues react when they saw him? He knew he would die there. But it wasn't March 28th. That was the only random coincidence that mattered to him anymore. He stopped walking, hesitant to do what he was about to do. Finally, he moved his feet and walked through the doors to the emergency room. His appearance caused neither concern nor interruption. If he had walked through the doors, strolled the entire waiting area, and left, most likely, no one would have even noticed him. Rachel Levy, the nurse with whom he had worked since the day he started in 2011, gave him the same consideration as every other spectator just looking to see what would happen next.

The digital clock on the wall read 12:01.

Saturday.

Everything was different, yet nothing had changed.

Chris sighed, then raised a hand to his temple as if rendering the world one final salute. With a smile on his face, he closed his eyes and softly whispered, "It's a great day when someone dies!"

IX - Saturday, April 5, 2014

Christopher J. Baxter, MD

Born: July 14, 1968, Beaverton, Oregon, United States of America

Place of death: Portland, Oregon, United States of America

Pak Ji-hyun

Born: April 3, 1996, Wonju, South Korea

Place of death: Seoul, South Korea

Zodi Dayak

Born: February 12, 1931, Timbuktu, Mali

Place of death: Kidal, Northern Mali

151,642 other souls worldwide

REQUIESCAT IN PACE

X - Thursday, April 7, 2016

VIRGINIA

Arlington National Cemetery

A picturesque springtime day was forming over the cemetery. The rising sun beamed across countless rows of white marble headstones, a solemn reminder of 152 years of history for the United States. So many tablets, each representing a unique life, now rested here together for a peaceful end. The day's interment was one more contribution.

Chris Baxter was by no means the first person to be buried at Arlington after the natural cycle of life and death resumed in the world.

On April 5, 2014, a young Army sergeant died in a training accident near Fort Riley, Kansas.

On September 26, 2014, Captain Benji Torim was shot and killed. After surviving a successful push in Marjah, Afghanistan, Torim had redeployed to Camp Lejeune, North Carolina, to reunite with his wife and finally meet his six-month-old son. That week, their photographs were published twice in the local newspaper. The first storybook shots captured the magic moment when Torim met his son for the first time. The second showed Candace holding Benji Jr. during his father's funeral. A sloppy gas station holdup had cut his life short.

Life was finally normal again—the natural order that we hate, despise...and need.

WONJU, SOUTH KOREA

For the next year, Kyle, who now preferred the name Pak Kun-hee, remained in Korea, mourning the loss of his daughter, Sarah, paying long-overdue respect to his wife, Mary, and believing that his rejection of his heritage had indirectly caused the loss of the two souls who mattered most to him. By staying in Wonju, he would not make the same mistake again. After Pak secured his nephew's early release from military service, Bung-ju worked for him as the assistant to the vice president of development.

Only after the *sosang*, a full year after Pak had laid his daughter to rest in the hillside grave beside his wife, did he resume the full scope of his job, working in both the US and South Korea. Bung-ju relocated to the United States to attend the University of North Carolina before returning as his uncle's protégé.

A GLOBAL RETURN TO NORMAL

By best estimates, 150,000 to 160,000 people died on April 5, 2014. This was a statistically normal number, by all measures.

- At 2:08 a.m., in San Antonio, Texas (12:08 a.m., Portland local time), a man passed away nine months after suffering a gunshot wound to the head.
- At 12:11 a.m., Sophia Doogan, a resident of Bakersfield, Calfornia, died peacefully in her sleep at the age of ninety-seven.
- At 10:31 a.m., in the border town of Arsal, Lebanon (12:31 a.m., Portland local time), a suicide bomber killed himself and three Lebanese soldiers after detonating a car bomb at an army checkpoint.
- Three people died at Saint Augustus Hospital in Portland, Oregon:
    - Cynthia Morgan, thirty-four, chronic obstructive lung disease
    - Gerard Kearns Anderson, sixty-eight, acute renal failure related to diabetes
    - Chris Baxter, forty-six, undetermined

Chris's cause of death remained undetermined, as did the cause of death of Porter Wilcox, fifty-one, the John Doe who had died on March 28 and was finally identified on April 5. He was a local Portland man with no known family. His neighbors could not tell the police much—they said he kept to himself. Also undetermined was why he went to Saint Augustus that night.

When Chris Baxter's death was reported, it was speculated that he was the first person in the world to die after "The Week" ended. Much like the last death, there was no way to prove such a claim. Government agencies and religious organizations were more interested in disproving it, but that was not possible either.

CHRISTOPHER J. BAXTER

After his death, Chris's body was seized by agents from the Centers for Disease Control and Prevention. In an attempt to determine his cause of death, his remains were tested and retested for every possible ailment or anomaly. They explored every physical, environmental, hereditary, chemical, viral, and biological possibility. When all tests came back negative, Chris's remains were retained, stored in abeyance, and monitored, "just to see" what might happen.

Chris's classmates from West Point, both those who were still in the military and those who were not, fought to have his remains released, and while outcry grew, it never gained a strong enough foothold to be successful. That changed at Scott Gipson's promotion ceremony on the River Entrance terrace of the Pentagon. Immediately following the ceremony, Brigadier General Gipson stormed into the office of the chairman of the Joint Chiefs of Staff and threw his freshly pinned star across the desk. Gipson's threat to walk away proved to be the impetus General Dell needed to reverse the decision. Out of respect for Chris's service, or perhaps out of fear of reprisal for disrespecting the now-global icon, Baxter was scheduled for burial at Arlington. Scotty and the rest of his classmates had little interest in the official reason. They just wanted a chance to bury their friend.

Arlington National Cemetery

In 2016, when March 28 to April 5 passed without incident for the second year in a row, Lieutenant Colonel Christopher Baxter was finally buried. His body was entombed in a lead-lined casket, sealed in concrete, placed in a metal vault, and lowered to its final location in Section 31. He lay next to the remains of SP4 Richard L.

McKinley, interred on January 25, 1961, a victim of a nuclear accident at the National Reactor Testing Station in Idaho Falls, Idaho. The burial was planned, announced, and conducted in less than two days. Graveside attendance was restricted. Chris Baxter had no family or friends in attendance except for the Reverend Susan Taple and 351 of his West Point classmates.

"When Chris passed away two years ago," Sue began, "I was with the group who helped collect his personal items and clean out what was left in his house after the Army cleared it." Those who were bitter over the bureaucratic reactions snickered and groaned. "This note is dated 28 March 2008. Chris wrote, 'Make sure my priest speaks at my funeral. Don't bury me on March 28th.' Well, Chris, I'm happy to let you know that Uncle Sam made sure your second request was met!" More chuckles and groans. "And as far as your priest, I don't know if it was me you had in mind, but here we are.

"I first met Chris just after his mother died. He called himself a lost soul who always felt there was something more he should have been doing with his life. His work as a doctor, his efforts to save lives—these things did not fulfill his desire to do more. Instead, they tormented him. His unselfish efforts made him believe that more and more was required of him. During what we now refer to as 'The Week,' Chris struggled to understand what it was he was supposed to do."

Sue knelt beside the disrupted ground and grabbed a handful of dirt before looking back up, tears streaming down her face.

"Nothing, Chris. You're not supposed to do anything more than what you have already done. I don't know if you played a part in The Week or not, but your story certainly did. Your story has been the focus of discussions around the world. Governments, churches, and communities use you as a beacon of what we all can do. Only time will tell if those beacons will hold their shine. There is nothing more you need to do; it's our turn now. We will remember your message, but I for one will never remember your day. Not everything has to have a connection."

After Sue closed her remembrance and prayed for the soul of her brother departed, she led the procession of Chris's classmates past the packed earth. The only words spoken were "Well done!" a solemn tribute to a soldier who emulated the tenets every West Point graduate holds dear: Duty, Honor, Country.

There were no guarantees for tomorrow.

Life returned to its former state.

Epilogue

So ends our tale. If you happen to look at a news site today, you'll see a most curious footnote:

A Farewell Note
by Colleen Fellow Peschel | March 28, 2053 at 4:25 PM

March 28, 2053 (UPI) --

My Dear Readers,

Reaching the end of a long career writing and sharing stories hardly warrants pity or compassion. I have pondered the finality of today's date for quite some time. Alas, now, with a tired soul, I pen a parting message to you before I switch from being a full-time reporter to being a full-time grandmother.

I awoke early this morning anticipating another lovely walk through the Crystal Springs Rhododendron Garden with my beautiful grandchildren by my side. Eleven years have passed since we were last graced with the enchantment of the rhododendrons' early springtime bloom. I have sung the praises of our magnificent garden here in Portland far too many times, but I ask for your consideration as I share one final moment.

Today, we adored the bright, mystical colors of our favorite blooms. Angelique loves violet blossoms, while sweet little John prefers fiery red. Both children ran from shrub to shrub, eager to hear the story the next color might bring. Every color has a story—a tale from the Fellow family past.

When we passed the orange florets, I paused to reflect on the many lifetimes they represent. My little darlings love to hear the stories my mother told me about Dad, whom they refer to as "your dad." I echo the vivid anecdotes Mother shared with me when I was a child, and do my best to imitate both the stern glares and boisterous laughs Dad often bounced between. John wants to grow up to be like my dad; I would like that. Angelique wishes she knew my dad; I wish the same.

For a moment, I paused to reflect on a few names I never share with my darlings. I thank Sam Baxter for the lessons he taught

Dad. I thank Chris Baxter for the lessons he taught me. Out there in the world is where I both tried to live my life according to the standards they both set. Here, among the orange rhododendrons, is the only place I mourn them.

Angelique and John could not understand why I was crying. I have never had the strength to tell them the story. As I stood there softly weeping, I took comfort in the only solace I needed: my loves holding me tight. They soothed my aching soul.

"It's okay, Grandma. Happy birthday!"

And so, for one last day, my friends, I whisper a fond adieu to the world.

~ Colleen

Colleen Fellow Peschel retires on her sixty-seventh birthday

(March 28, 1986 -)

Sources

While *...in abeyance* is a work of fiction, it is aligned with actual events of historical significance and peppered with my personal accumulation of memories, stories, and research. I have elected to organize the sources I consulted by storyline rather than by chapter.

THE TRAGIC TALE OF JOHN DOE

Advanced Life Support Group, "The Management of Cardiac Arrest," in *Advanced Paediatric Life Support: The Practical Approach*, eds., Martin Samuels, and Susan Wieteska (Wiley-Blackwell, 2011), 47–56a, http://www.alsg.org/en/files/Ch06_CA2006.pdf.

THE TRAGIC TALE OF SAM BAXTER

"History of DNA Testing," DNA Diagnostics Center, accessed May 19, 2018, http://www.dnacenter.com/science-technology/dna-history-1980.html.

Theresa McKinlay, "MAX Light-Rail Service Begins in 1986," *Daily Journal of Commerce, Oregon*, September 16, 2008, http://djcoregon.com/news/2008/09/16/max-lightrail-service-begins-in-1986/.

"Thirty Years of HIV/AIDS: Snapshots of an Epidemic," amfAR, The Foundation for AIDS Research, accessed April 22, 2014, http://www.amfar.org/thirty-years-of-hiv/aids-snapshots-of-an-epidemic/.

THE TRAGIC TALE OF PAK JI-HYUN

Constantine Sarkos,"Research-Derived Aircraft Fire Safety Improvements (2000–2010)," Society of Fire Protection Engineers (SFPE), *Fire Protection Engineering*, no. 1 (2013), http://www.sfpe.org/?page=2013_Q1_4.

"Report on Development and Operation of Incheon International Airport," International Civil Aviation Organization: Facilitation (FAL) Division, March 15, 2004, http://www.icao.int/Meetings/FAL12/Documents/fal12ip017_en.pdf.

THE TRAGIC TALE OF CAPTAIN BENJI TORIM

Bryant Jordan, "General: Marines Ready to Leave Helmand Province," Military.com, accessed April 21, 2014, http://www.military.com/daily-news/2014/03/06/general-marines-ready-to-leave-helmand-province.html.

THE GLORIOUS TALE OF ZODI DAYAK AND THE CHILDREN OF MALI

"Regional Overview: Sub-Saharan Africa," United Nations Educational, Scientific and Cultural Organization (UNESCO), accessed April 21, 2014, http://en.unesco.org/gem-report/sites/gem-report/files/157229E.pdf.

Mark Eveleigh, "Surviving the Sahara: Three Weeks with the Tuareg," CNN Travel, March 24, 2013, http://travel.cnn.com/surviving-sahara-468896.

Reuters, "Tribal Chief of Mali's Tuaregs Dies Amid Stalled Peace Talks," December 18, 2014, http://www.reuters.com/article/2014/12/18/us-mali-tuareg-idUSKBN0JW2TA20141218.

"Mali," Countries and Their Cultures, *World Culture Encyclopedia*, accessed June 17, 2015. http://www.everyculture.com/Ja-Ma/Mali.html.

Wikipedia Contributors, "Tuareg People," *Wikipedia, The Free Encyclopedia*, accessed May 20, 2018, https://en.wikipedia.org/w/index.php?title=Tuareg_people&oldid=840745832.

SCOTT GIPSON IN THAILAND

"Timeline: Events in the Lead-up to Thailand's Political Unrest," The ABC (Australian Broadcasting Corporation), last modified May 23, 2014, http://www.abc.net.au/news/2014-02-04/timeline-of-the-lead-up-to-thailands-political-unrest/5234094.

COLLEEN FELLOW FROM THE *PORTLAND TIMES*

J. Mark Garber, "Look for Your New Tribune on Tuesdays," *Portland Tribune,* February 13, 2014, http://portlandtribune.com/pt/9-news/210594-68351-look-for-your-new-tribune-on-tuesdays.

Donald Olson, "Crystal Springs Rhododendron Garden," *Frommer's,* accessed April 23, 2014, http://www.frommers.com/destinations/portland-or/attractions/873486.

"The Portland Chapter American Rhododendron Society," Portland Chapter, American Rhododendron Society, accessed April 23, 2014, http://www.rhodies.org/.

WORLD POPULATION STATISTICS AND DEATH RATES

"World Birth and Death Rates," Ecology Global Network, accessed April 21, 2014, http://www.ecology.com/birth-death-rates.

"Population Estimates for Oregon and Counties," Portland State University, Population Research Center, December 15, 2013, https://pdxscholar.library.pdx.edu/populationreports/34.

"The Top 10 Causes of Death," World Health Organization, February 28, 2017, http://www.who.int/mediacentre/factsheets/fs310/en/index2.html.

"Fast Facts on U.S. Hospitals, 2018," *AHA Hospital Statistics, 2018,* American Hospital Association, accessed May 19, 2018, https://www.aha.org/statistics/fast-facts-us-hospitals.

"Live Births, Deaths, and Infant Deaths, Latest Available Year (2002-2016)," Population and Vital Statistics Report, United Nations Statistics Division, last modified January 2, 2018, http://unstats.un.org/unsd/demographic/products/vitstats/serATab3.pdf.

CHRIS BAXTER: BACKSTORY

Wikipedia Contributors, "Battle of Basra (2008)," *Wikipedia, The Free Encyclopedia,* accessed May 20, 2018, https://en.wikipedia.org/w/index.php?title=Battle_of_Basra_(2008)&oldid=833707987.

GLOBAL CHAOS OF "THE EVENT"

"Independent States in the World," U.S. Department of State, April 11, 2017, http://www.state.gov/s/inr/rls/4250.htm.

Stephanie Serna, "SA Man Dies 9 Months After Being Shot: Medical Examiner Rules Death of David Koah a Homicide," KSAT, January 14, 2015, https://www.ksat.com/news/sa-man-dies-9-months-after-being-shot.

Reuters, "Car Bomb Kills Three Soldiers in Attack on Lebanese Army Checkpoint," *Chicago Tribune*, March 29, 2014, http://articles.chicagotribune.com/2014-03-29/news/sns-rt-us-lebanon-violence-20140327_1_car-bomb-three-soldiers-arsal.

"Death Notices for Saturday, March 29, 2014," *Porterville Recorder*, March 29, 2014, http://www.recorderonline.com/news/local_news/death-notices-for-saturday-march/article_f1a01750-b6e2-11e3-88a5-001a4bcf6878.html.

"End of Time Prophecies, Apocalypse & Eschatology," Discovering Islam, April 23, 2014, http://www.discoveringislam.org/end_of_time.htm.

Jay Solomon, and Carol E. Lee, "Obama Wrote Secret Letter to Iran's Khamenei about Fighting Islamic State," *Wall Street Journal*, November 6, 2014, https://www.marketwatch.com/story/obama-wrote-secret-letter-to-irans-khameni-about-fighting-islamic-state-2014-11-07.

Associated Press, "Obama Sends 100 Troops to Combat LRA in Uganda," *Guardian*, October 14, 2011, http://www.theguardian.com/world/2011/oct/14/obama-sends-troops-uganda.

THE FINAL RESTING PLACE OF CHRIS BAXTER

"Richard Leroy McKinley, Specialist 4th Class, United States Army," last modified July 25, 2006, http://www.arlingtoncemetery.net/rlmckinl.htm.

The Completely Inconsequential Ramblings of a Condemned Man

inconsequential

adjective

inconsequential (*comparative* more inconsequential, *superlative* most inconsequential)

1. Having no consequence; not consequential; of little importance.
2. Not logically following from the premises.

inconsequential. (2018, February 12). Wiktionary, The Free Dictionary. Retrieved 22:38, April 26, 2018 from https://en.wiktionary.org/w/index.php?title=inconsequential&oldid=48988565.

* * *

Your support will help define the importance of my words. Please donate today at: Main.NationalMSSociety.org/goto/EMBK.
Because it is a fight.
For approximately 2.3 million people with MS worldwide, the fight is not over and it won't be over until a cure is found.

It will never stop...nor will we
It will never quit...nor will we
This is why we fight!

Never Stop... Never Quit...®
NeverStopNeverQuit.com

This book is dedicated to us, our loved ones, and our supporters. Thank you for the motivation every day.

Acknowledgment

The symptoms listed, and their corresponding descriptions at the end of each chapter, are quoted directly from the National MS Society > SYMPTOMS & DIAGNOSIS > MS SYMPTOMS.

For a complete list of symptoms and additional resources, please go to the source: NationalMSSociety.org/Symptoms-Diagnosis/MS-Symptoms.

I - Inconsequential Ramblings...

"This is not going to end well for me, is it?" (channeling my best *Deadpool)*

As I face the incessant onslaught of multiple sclerosis (MS), there are only a few options for my next move:

- Roll over and give up.
- Maintain a blind, nothing-but-rosy outlook.
- Keep fighting the best way I know how: by telling stories about my shortcomings while battling MS, doing so in a

way that best captures my pain and loss and also helps me maintain my loose grip on sanity—with satire.

I like the last option, so that's what I'll do.

"You can't make fun of disability! It's not funny."

"Bulls#%t! I think it's hysterical, and I can prove it," (channeling my best George Carlin).

So, join me in my adventure as I attempt to describe the suck, pain, loss, and the hilarity of life with MS.

Disclaimer: The pessimistic and sarcastic views presented in this piece belong, of course, solely to me. Everyone's experience is unique to their specific circumstances-not everyone will find my way of looking at things funny. Right now, to preserve the few remaining snippets of my sanity, I really don't have any other option. Also, please don't be angry with my friends and family because I'm an ass. It's not their fault.

II - Numbness and Other Inconsequential Ramblings of a Condemned Man

I lost my keys the other day. If they're not in one of three locations—on my nightstand, the kitchen island, or in my gym bag—a scavenger hunt is sure to ensue.

Brie gave me a handy Tile tracker chip for my key ring. Lost your keys? Press *Locate* on your phone app and a ring will alert you to the location of your misplaced keys. It works in reverse as well: press the Tile chip, find your phone. Great concept. The problem is, I only receive alerts when I accidentally press the *Locate* button on the Tile chip as I am leaving the house, keys and phone both in hand. My friendly phone rings, alerting me that my phone is right there in my right hand. I can't feel it (I've had limited feeling in that hand since 1999), but because I am staring at the damn phone, I'm already well aware of the fact.

Why can't I just have a regular place to put my keys every time? Like a nightstand, a kitchen island, or maybe a gym bag? Once, when Brie put my keys on the key hook in our kitchen, I couldn't find them for four hours.

On this particular day, I needed my keys immediately. With a halfhearted commitment to what I knew could be a fruitless effort, I activated the app on my phone. No beep, no chirp. The adventure began [cue slapstick music]. Nightstand? Nope. Kitchen island? Sorry. Gym bag? Strike three! Laundry hamper, gym bag, pants pockets (yesterday's), dog bed, living room cushions, kitchen island, pants pockets (currently wearing), Ellie's room, nightstand, hallway, driveway, car (unlocked, no keys), gym bag, nightstand? I surrender.

"They'll show up!" I relied upon the most optimistic justification for failure in the English language. I decided to pass the time with frivolous activities, hoping my keys would simply materialize. After cleaning up clutter for about ten minutes, I grabbed my gym bag to move it to its designated spot on the floor.

My keys fell out.

I found them in the second-to-last place I looked.

It was also the third place.

And the fifth.

I'm still learning how to be disabled, hanging on to a former life, hoping my body will rediscover what my mind still finds normal.

Stick my hand in the pocket of my bag and fish around for the keys. That should work, right? I have three jingly keys, three rings, and a square Tile tracker attached. It doesn't work because I can't feel anything with my right hand. Nevertheless, I adhere to obsolete routines. Maybe I'll hear the keys jingle, or maybe I'll feel the cold metal on one of the random spots on my hand where I occasionally have sensation. I prefer to hope for one or both of these possibilities rather than to dump out a bag full of junk on the off-chance my keys will magically appear on top of the pile.

Great, more clutter.

I should get a Tile.

* * *

Numbness of the face, body, or extremities (arms and legs) is often the first symptom experienced by those eventually diagnosed as having MS.

III - Incontinence and Other Inconsequential Ramblings of a Condemned Man

Once again, just the other day, I was Eleanor's hero.

SUPER DADDY on the way, able to rescue a scared little girl in a single bound!

The poor kid had an accident during the night. She was upset the next morning and tried to explain that she didn't do anything wrong. I figured it was time to fess up. "Hey, sweetie, it's okay. It was just an accident. It happens to everyone when they're growing up. I've had accidents, too."

"Really?"

"Yep. I've had accidents outside. I peed in my pants while I was just walking around. It happens sometimes."

"Wow! How old were you when that happened?"

"Forty-five."

I really hope my daughter doesn't have a poop accident. I don't want to have to tell *that* story.

* * *

Bladder dysfunction, which occurs in at least 80% of people with MS, can usually be managed quite successfully with medications, fluid management, and intermittent self-catheterization.

IV - Cognitive Changes and Other Inconsequential Ramblings of a Condemned Man

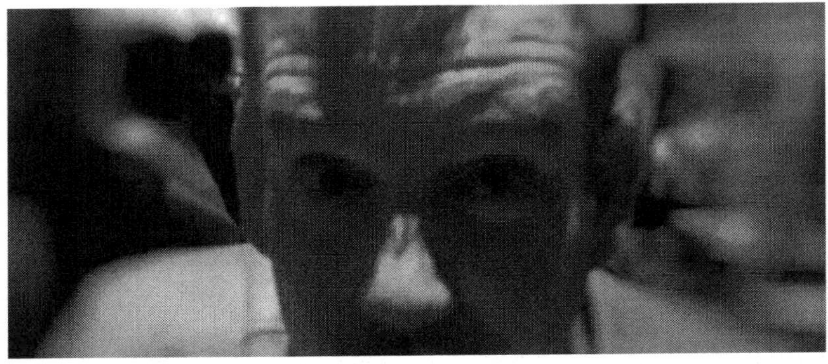

One of the most electrifying elements of Bike MS—our annual fundraising event with the National MS Society—is the opportunity to gather every year with an army of Team Amulet riders, reunite with teammates from the past, and welcome exciting new faces.

A few years ago, I met one of our new faces on the first day. I guessed she was probably one of the riders recruited by Brie. So, being the Mr. Outgoing Personality I am, I hopped over to introduce myself. "Hi! Welcome to the team. I'm Kevin, Brie's husband." Upon hearing her gentle response, Mr. Outgoing Personality shrunk to about two feet.

"Kevin, I've ridden on your team for the past three years. If you introduce yourself one more time, I'm going to smack you."

Points noted: We've met before, I've done this before, never again forget that your name is...I can't remember.

Cognitive issues are common in MS patients. I'm fortunate, in a sense, because my memory remains strong in most areas. I'm on the board of directors for three nonprofits, my financial analysis acumen rivals Warren Buffett's. In fact, we differ in only two areas: $50 billion and the ability to remember the names of people we met five minutes ago.

Damn, I'm so close.

I am married to an outgoing, gotta-meet-new-people person. My daughter is a social butterfly who already has more close friends than I've accumulated in my lifetime. Once my dog gets a sniff of you, and she approves, you are forever in her heart and mind. Then there's me, the recluse who hates social gatherings. We went to a fundraiser for Eleanor's school a few weeks ago. There were over one hundred people at the event; I should have known thirty or more; at least thirty-five or forty knew me; when I showed up, I could name maybe six or seven; I met another ten to fifteen new people. I think I forgot one or two names over the course of the evening, leaving slightly more ignorant than when I arrived.

It's not, "Yeah, I have trouble remembering people's names." It's a therapist-level, neurologist-level condition. My regular doctors (I kind of remember their names) cannot pinpoint a specific cause or treatment. I have undergone a variety of tests with several Dr. WhatTheHellWereTheirNames; my retention and recall are superb—except for those gaps.

It's terrifying to stand in a familiar room and feel utterly disconnected. When Brie and I go out with people from my social circle (gatherings where innocent folk are damned to be classified in the same group as me), her rude, inconsiderate jerk of a husband never introduces her to others. She's forced to announce herself and become acquainted with them on her own. I merely agree I'm rude while I scold myself, "Aaaah, that's their name. Dammit, I should've remembered that. I'll remember now." My vow, of course, lasts about five minutes.

There is no pattern. Old friends, new friends, no matter. Coworkers, family members, and neighbors are all fair game. Long-term memory is better than short, so if you have known me for forty-five years, hopefully I'll give you more than a "Hey 'sup!" Unfortunately, it's not a given.

I'm trapped on the periphery of life, an unwanted man looking into a world only slightly familiar. There are days when it's scary as hell to run into someone, a person I may know or should know, and have no clue what my relationship is to the figure standing before me. With luck, I have an idea where we know each other from (Eleanor's school, old work, neighborhood), but I just cannot recall their name.

So, the next time we run into each other somewhere/anywhere, and I give you the "Hey! How's it going?" please be kind. I'm not rude (intentionally), I'm not an ass (this time), I don't think I'm above you (at least not until I get my $50 billion). There is a good chance I just don't remember your name.

* * *

Cognitive Changes refers to a range of high-level brain functions affected in more than 50% of people with MS, including the ability to process incoming information, learn and remember new information, organize and problem-solve, focus attention and accurately perceive the environment.

V - Weakness and Other Inconsequential Ramblings of a Condemned Man

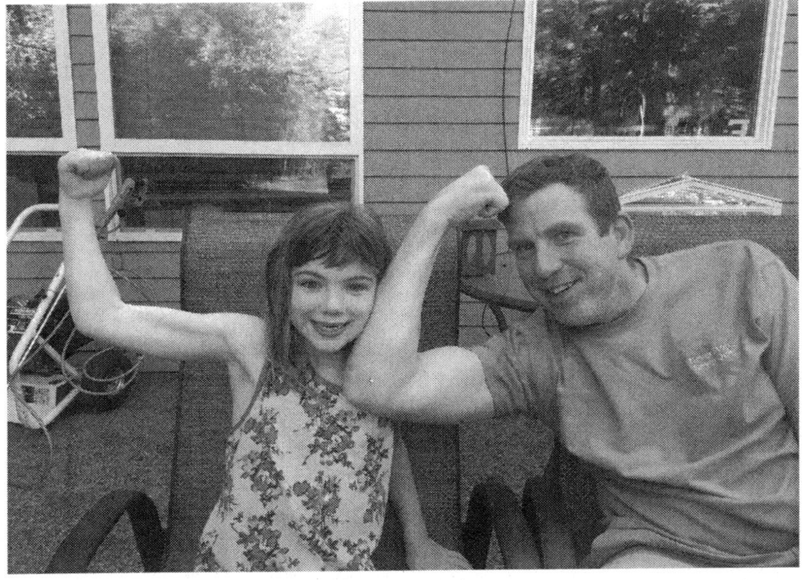

Let's try an experiment. (Trust me, I know what I'm doing; I write a blog.) Take a thirty-pound weight in one hand and hold it using only the tips of your fingers. Stand up and let the arm holding the weight hang by your side. Your fingers are slightly curled, unable to fully extend (or you would drop the weight), yet you can't quite curl them enough to make them a fist.

The test here is not to accomplish this feat, although it is tricky, but rather to see what else you can do with your now-encumbered limb. Try to live. Take a shot at getting out of bed, donning your slippers, walking the dog (heck, clipping the leash to her collar), taking a shower, washing your hair, brushing your teeth, combing your hair, dressing (including buttoning and zipping your pants), putting on socks, tying your shoes.

This experiment replicates the issues I face. Every day, I try to do this with my dominant arm—the one in which I have tactile sensation, but also fading strength in—not the one I can move easily but have limited feeling in and control of. In addition to the awkwardness, this is the amount of function and level of difficulty I have with my left arm. The eyesore hangs limp much of the time; my fingers can't ball up but will not fully extend; with everything I do, it feels as if I am living with a thirty-pound weight hanging from my fingertips. It is weak all the time, tires quickly, and continues to worsen. Because the nerve cells do not "fire" correctly in this arm, I cannot move it well. Because I cannot move my arm well, I don't use it as much. Because I don't use it as much, it continues to weaken. Because my arm continues to weaken, I cannot move it well...and so on. And no, the feeling of having this extra weight does not magically help me build muscle. My arm just gets weaker.

Well, that sucks.

I still try to use my arm as much as possible. Just today, I picked up a piece of paper from the floor all by myself, although I needed my right arm to pat myself on the back afterward.

My situation is bad. As atrophy sets in, it worsens by the day. My options are fairly limited at the moment, so the best I can do is to try to maintain the muscle tone and overall flexibility I still have. Use it or lose it, as they say.

My physical therapist directed a regimen of upper-body exercises to do with resistance bands or with the cable-pulling machine at the gym. It's a pretty good workout for my right side, pushing the limits of my strength and range of motion. When doing these exercises with my left arm, my body whimpers with the slightest amount of weight, down to and including zero pounds. The looks I get are interesting. Sometimes, when I'm standing in front of the machine performing a split-stance, single-arm cable chest press without any cable or weight, I just want to yell out, "What's the matter, you've never seen a man pumping air before?"

Nevertheless, I continue my workouts to reduce the rate of decay on my left side while strengthening my core and right side; I notice significant changes on both; my dwindling, ten-and-a-half-inch left bicep versus my uncontrollable eighteen-inch, gorilla-strength right.

I need my left arm. I just wouldn't feel right without it.

* * *

Weakness in MS, which results from deconditioning of unused muscles or damage to nerves that stimulate muscles, can be managed with rehabilitation strategies and the use of mobility aids and other assistive devices.

VI - Vision and Other Inconsequential Ramblings of a Condemned Man

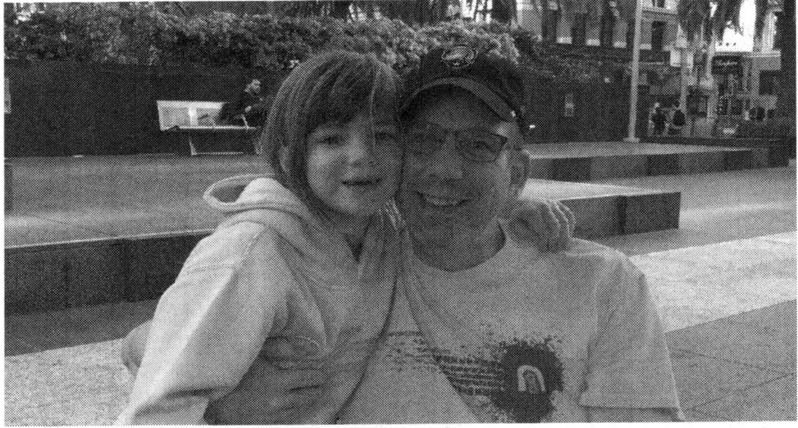

Soon after sliding into secondary progressive MS, I started having a problem with my eyes. My adventure began with a trip to the eye clinic for a full examination. I was amazed by the deterioration I had experienced in such a short period of time: I had gone down two levels on a standardized eye chart. At the end of the exam, my optometrist broke the bad news: "Your vision is 20/20."

"Damn! This is what 20/20 looks like? That sucks."

Now, my vision ranges from 20/20, to 20/30, to 20/crappy, waxing and waning all the time. The only number I'll never have again is the 20/10 of my glorious pilot days. The last ophthalmologist I saw was surprised I was ever able to fly in the first place. Apparently, double vision is not all that common. Take a stereogram (two-dimensional pictures that can create three-dimensional images) as an example. Look at the picture and relax your eyes. The images you see will seem to separate, and when they overlap, another image will appear.

This was never a problem for me. I always saw double. I have an irregular setting of my eye sockets. However, the muscles in my eyes were always strong enough to compensate for my double vision. Like so many of my other muscles, now these too are failing as a result of my MS.

I shouldn't complain, I guess. I do have the provocative allure of my displaced ocular canals (lookout, ladies!)]. Plus, my eyesight isn't bad all the time. It tends to fail in spurts.

1999: Blurred vision in my right eye was one of the initial symptoms of the first MS attack.

2002: Inability to focus my eyes led to my first experiment with glasses (it failed).

2005: I called and left a message for Brie, saying, "I can't see out of my right eye, so I'm driving myself to the hospital. Can you meet me there?" Relapse.

2009: KB the Pirate showed up to work one day with a patch over his right eye. The next day, I showed up with the patch over my left eye. This was the first time I was unable to merge the two images, from both eyes, so we removed one at a time.

2011: To address my ever-changing vision, I tried wearing prism glasses (it failed). If you want to make yourself throw up in five minutes, wait four minutes and forty seconds, put on a pair of prism glasses—and then stand up.

2014: My vision officially sucks (although the nurse started to fall for those sexy ocular canals).

2016: I now have two pairs of glasses for when my vision passes through a particular range of suck. When I need them, I pray to God they are within reach (usually, they aren't).

I am fortunate. My MS diagnosis does not include optic neuritis (possibly), and my eyes do not have a constant stinging pain (usually). I am mostly cursed with middle-aged eyes and an MS condition where I can no longer compensate for my displaced ocular canals...my disease can no longer control my deformity.

Well, doesn't that just double suck.

* * *

Vision Problems are the first symptom of MS for many people. Onset of blurred vision, poor contrast or color vision, and pain on eye movement can be frightening–and should be evaluated promptly.

VII - Speech and Other Inconsequential Ramblings of a Condemned Man

Me: (inaudible grumble mumble, mumble grumble)

Brie: "What?"

Me: (inaudible grumble mumble, mumble grumble)

Brie: "What?"

Me: "Eleanor, tell your mother what I just said, please."

Eleanor: "Daddy said he was going to the store to get some milk. Do you need anything else?"

Brie: "No."

Me: (inaudible grumble mumble, mumble grumble)

E: "He will be back in about ten minutes."

Brie: "Okay. Have fun."

Me: (inaudible grumble mumble, mumble grumble)

In my normal state, I sound and walk like a drunken frat boy stumbling home on Saturday night. In other words, I mumble, I stumble, fall regularly, and generally move around as if I'm intoxicated. I spend a lot of time convincing people I'm okay.

I've been cut off in bars before I ordered my first drink.

When I was working, there were several complaints submitted to Human Resources about me being drunk at the office.

I see the stares and overhear what people who don't know me are saying, especially if I have a beer in my hand.

My slurred speech does not present a physical danger to me, as many other symptoms of my MS do. More than anything, my speech causes me to stay away from large crowds of people. It kills me to think there are parents who, seeing me when we're out, ask, "What the hell is up with Eleanor's dad?" Friends and family members who spend a decent amount of time around me can usually understand what I am saying, although there are always those times...those who haven't spent much time with me may not comprehend my words so well, but they understand my basket of issues. Eleanor, My Little Love, is the only person to whom I have never needed to repeat myself (except for when her nose is buried in an iPad and I get the occasional, "huuuuh?"). She doesn't know Daddy any other way; to her, this is normal.

So, if you see me out somewhere and I look like I've had a few too many, please feel free to ask me if that's what is going on. If you still think I've had too much to drink, stick around for a while, have four or five delicious IPAs with me, and if my slurring and stumbling get worse, I wasn't drunk when we first ran into each other.

* * *

Speech problems, including slurring (dysarthria) and loss of volume (dysphonia) occur in approximately 25-40% of people with MS, particularly later in the disease course and during periods of extreme fatigue. Stuttering is occasionally reported as well.

VIII - Gait and Other Inconsequential Ramblings of a Condemned Man

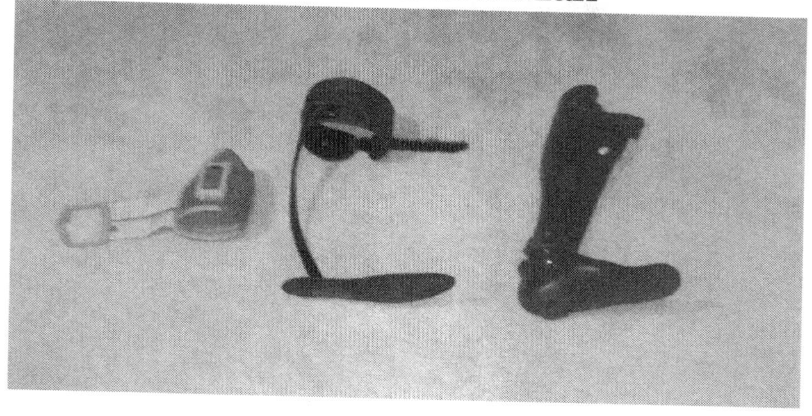

This is, without a doubt, the most observable of my MS symptoms. If you see me sitting down, eating or chatting, you may not notice anything unusual about me. But when I stand up and start to walk, that's when you'll notice something is going on. It may look like I am doing a feeble imitation of a zombie or a walker—and there is nothing graceful about it. I am slow, I fall regularly, and walking takes an immense amount of energy. Most of my most significant injuries are the result of falls. (I wonder, would Brie have signed on so readily if I had included this in my Match.com profile?)

Walking is difficult, but I am going to walk. There's no debating this. To keep this commitment, I need a lot of help. I would like to introduce you to my walking aids. They are prominently featured in what I like to call my Summer 2017 Mobility Fashion line [cue runway sequence.]

High Performance

If you're looking for top-line results, look no further than the Bioness L300. Designed with performance in mind, the L300 will exceed your every expectation. This brace isn't for the faint of heart; if you're like me and have a sensitivity to deep pulses of electricity shooting through your leg, you need to use this brace in well-planned, manageable chunks. When you do, the rewards are plentiful.

No matter if you are walking to defeat MS,

walking the dog,

or walking around the dance floor with your little love,

you are walking on sunshine with the Bioness L300! (Bioness is a proud sponsor of Team Amulet and Bike MS 2017.)

Utility

This brace will get you anywhere you want to go. It's the perfect concoction of mediocrity: it can do "just about everything," but only just a bit. Light, durable, and accommodating, this ankle-foot orthosis (AFO) is a simple, easy, fire-and-forget solution. Wear it all day,

wear it around the house,

on the beach,

or on the moon.

A utility AFO is essential for day-to-day living.

MOAB

The "Mother of All Braces" is as indestructible as you were before you were diagnosed with MS. There's nothing this brace can't do, nowhere it can't go. It's tough on your body, but if that's what it takes to be immortal...

If you wear the MOAB, you had better be on the move, for it doesn't like to sit still. Your leg will regret a sedentary lifestyle. "It" has no emotion. You must bring personality to the game yourself. I suggest a matching ensemble.

NEVER
QUIT

Trekking Pole

If it's a trekking pole, you're an athlete, not a cripple. Mind over matter.

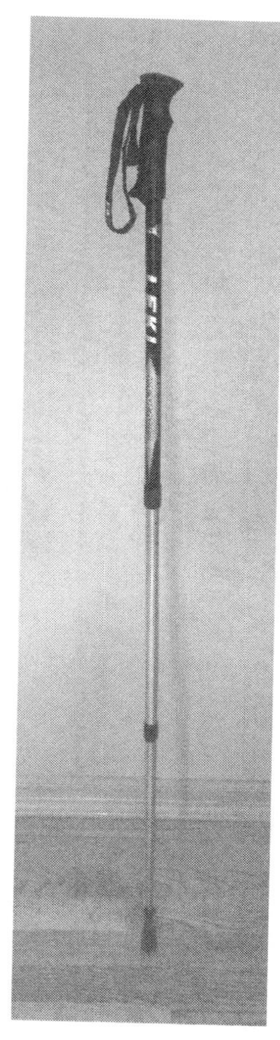

Canes

If you must go the traditional route, do it with style. Add a little flair to your repertoire. Black is run-down and beaten. Today, we got pinks, we got blues, we got sexy curves, we got built-in stands for those who don't want to waste time "putting something down."

Just remember, you don't have to do this alone.

* * *

Walking (Gait) Difficulties are related to several factors including weakness, spasticity, loss of balance, sensory deficit and fatigue, and can be helped by physical therapy, assistive therapy and medications.

IX - Pain
and Other Inconsequential Ramblings of a Condemned Man

Please don't try this at home.

Stick your hand into an open flame. Does it hurt?

Now, leave it there. If the pain doesn't get worse—and if you somehow knew you wouldn't suffer irreparable damage from being dumb enough to stick your hand in the middle of an open flame—could you keep it there? And if so, for how long?

One minute?

Five minutes?

My hand has been stuck in the middle of the open flame for almost eighteen years.

It is said that all things are relative, including pain. That's true...to a certain point. If you continuously have pain without any other physical repercussions, the pain becomes normalized. The pain will only "hurt" (for lack of a better description) if it worsens or if you think about it.

Over time, I grew accustomed to that ever-present pain, comfortable with the fact that my pain threshold was only being exceeded one or two times per month. Then, my MS developed into secondary progressive MS. My "relative" pain is now everywhere: arms, legs, head, chest...

Relatively speaking, this pain sucks.

The ancient Roman poet Ovid is credited with having said, "Endure and persist; this pain will turn to good by and by." I, personally, would like to smack the individual who translated Ovid's quote this way. Clearly, this person never endured Mr. Pitula's high school Latin class.

"Perfer et obdura! dolor hic tibi proderit olim" (Ovid, Amores. 3.11a. 7-8).

A better translation is, "Bear and persist! The suffering will be useful to you." (Thank you, George, for teaching me the proper syntax, conjugations, and declensions.)

Suffering builds character. It provides you with the means to develop a moral code to live your life by. It teaches you how to use life's challenges to rise above and improve. Pain teaches you three things: pain sucks, don't do what you did, and bury your pain if you want to live. Lesson learned. Don't get MS.

For so many reasons, my suffering will be useful to me. I will use it to leave my influence in the world. If I could remove one thing from this Life Lesson that is my MS, it would be pain. Physical pain, especially when there is little hope of it subsiding, can quickly drive even the healthiest of men to take desperate measures.

* * *

Pain syndromes are common in MS. In one study, 55% of people with MS had "clinically significant pain" at some time, and almost half had chronic pain.

X - Swallowing and Other Inconsequential Ramblings of a Condemned Man

I have never had someone spit their drink in my face, even though, admittedly, I have deserved it on several occasions. No, you have to screw up royally to have someone spit their drink in your face. It is a public shaming spectacle, reserved only for the most egregious of behaviors. Once, a buddy of mine, in the middle of a restaurant, in front of our wives, committed the greatest of sins.

He sat across from me.

Man, did he get soaked! From the chest up. Luckily, I was only drinking water at the time.

When you swallow, there is a distinct rhythm and sequence to the movement of the muscles, cartilage, and tissue of the throat. Here's a breakdown of the three phases of swallowing, as well as where my body fails:

Phase 1: This is the oral phase. It consists of biting and chewing. The most significant issue I have with this phase has nothing to do with MS. It's eating my food like I am a damn seventeen-year-old plebe at West Point again (big bites, three chews, and one swallow).

Phase 2: This is the pharyngeal phase. The epiglottis closes over the top of the larynx, preventing food and liquid from going into the lungs. My muscles often fail to time this maneuver effectively. I've watched an x-ray video of myself swallowing (it's called a video fluoroscopic swallowing exam). When I swallow, some of it goes into my lungs. Sometimes it's just a bit, other times it's a shitload (FYI, inhaling a "shitload" of anything is not good for you). My doctor tried to console me by pointing out that because I am young(ish) and can cough up and expel whatever I happen to aspirate into my lungs, it isn't that much of a (physical) problem for me. But, as I age, or if something unusual happens, my ability to expel will decrease, thereby increasing my chances of developing aspiration pneumonia (caused by bacteria growing in the lungs from inhaled food and liquid). That was not much of a consolation.

Note #1: I have a doctor's note and corroborating video evidence for my sideshow skit of spitting food and beverage all over the place. I apologize profusely.

Note #2: This is easily on my top-five list of "MS Things That Are Probably Going to Kill Me." I'm thinking of starting my own deadpool.

Phase 3: There is a coordinated rhythm to the muscles that move food down the esophagus and to the stomach. I already know I ain't got no rhythm, so there's no need for my MS to remind me constantly. Yet, still, it does. About ten or twelve times a day, my esophagus misfires. For example, when taking a delicious bite of Brie's chicken casserole, it gets lodged in my throat. This is usually not that much of a problem because I can wait for the muscles to resync or drink a sip of something to wash it down.

Inside Voice: "Great plan, moron."

Outside Voice: "Thanks!"

Inside Voice: "You forgot about the issues."

Outside Voice: "What issues?"

Inside Voice: "The fact that while your esophagus is swallowing, your epiglottis is covering the larynx, and that prevents breathing. Or, the fact that food pressed against your esophagus can become lodged or stuck, even after normal swallowing resumes, continuing your coughing and breathing fiasco?"

Outside Voice: "Oh, yeah! I forgot about that. That's bad."

* * *

Swallowing problems–referred to as dysphagia–result from damage to the nerves controlling the many small muscles in the mouth and throat.

XI - Spasticity and Other Inconsequential Ramblings of a Condemned Man

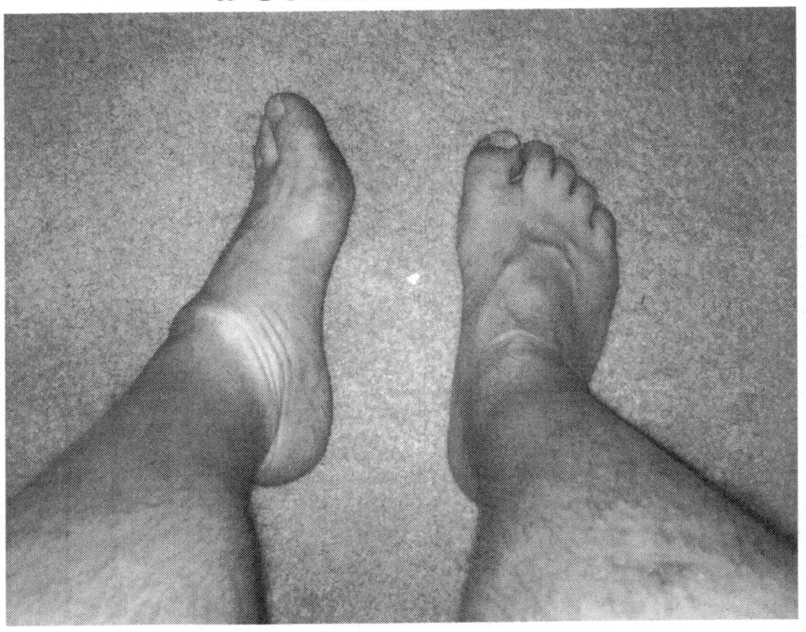

"Spaz!"

I never hear anyone use the word "spaz" anymore. I don't hear it on TV either. Maybe it was just a 70s term. Of course, the decline in usage of a derogatory term is never a bad thing. I must confess, I'm guilty of using it. I still chuckle when I hear the word.

"Spaz!"

[Hee-hee]

See? The word still makes me laugh, even if I'm poking fun at myself.

"Hi, my name is Kevin, and I am a spaz."

[Hee-hee]

To express my predicament in a more politically correct fashion, I suffer from varying degrees of spasticity. It is a direct result of having MS. This symptom, which has plagued me since the onset of my disease in 1999, has presented itself in a variety of forms. As with many of my issues, unfortunately, this too is worsening.

First, it was cool.

I was in command of an air cavalry troop station in Korea when I was first diagnosed. I was immediately grounded, never to fly helicopters again, but I remained in-country for another nine months. My troop mission was maintenance and repair of the Apache helicopters assigned to our squadron, a job I was still able to perform.

For me, there was nothing like serving as a troop commander at Camp Eagle (Wonju, Korea). With 135 soldiers under my command, I was a big fish in a little pond. Our tiny camp held the airfield, hangar, barracks, and a bar. There wasn't much do in Korea other than work and drink, and I was quite proficient at both! As the commander, I often had the chance to drink with my soldiers. Nothing says, "I am the Commander, the Big Cheese, the HMFIC," like sitting in a bar, decked out in your flight suit and Cav Stetson, when your hand grip spasms, shattering the highball glass you're holding, splattering blood down your hand, and showing no reaction, no emotion at all ("I ain't got time to bleed"). Compared to the other problems I was having, this one wasn't so bad.

Later on, it was an annoyance.

Muscle spasms, mostly in my calves, had already been plaguing me for years. Because my MS symptoms were generally mild at the time, the leg cramps, while bothersome, were not a main focus of my treatment. Lots of people gave me suggestions though.

"You should eat more bananas. Are you eating bananas? If you are, you're not eating enough bananas!"

Outside Voice: "Stop saying banana!"

Inside Voice: "Banana, banana, banana."

"You should drink tonic water. That will get rid of your cramps. Drink lots of tonic water." By the way, I hate tonic water.

Once, when I was staying at a friend's parents' house, I woke up in the middle of the night because I felt something in the bed. *What the hell is that?* It was a bar of soap underneath the mattress cover.

"That'll get rid of the cramps in your legs."

Just no.

Now, it is crippling. I wake up in the morning with such severe spasms in my foot and ankle, I can't do a thing. Do you have any idea how difficult it is to walk on your ankle?

Also, my leg braces are not always effective. My L300, designed to supplement the damaged nerves and weakened muscles that have caused foot drop, cannot compensate for the strength of the opposite spasming muscle. My utility AFO is just too flimsy to overcome the deformation caused by involuntary spasms. The MOAB is great–if I can actually straighten my leg enough to get my foot in the brace.

Spasms in my left hand cause my fingers to ball up into a fist, so much so that my hand becomes useless: a weak, underpowered, dead stump with a fist-ball hanging from the end.

Spasms in my bladder can have unpleasant consequences, from "I can't pee," to "please stop peeing," and this happens at random, inconvenient moments.

Out-of-nowhere spasms in my chest, neck, arms, and abdomen can make me look like...well...a spaz!

[Hee-hee]

* * *

Spasticity refers to feelings of stiffness and a wide range of involuntary muscle spasms; can occur in any limb, but it is much more common in the legs.

XII - Vertigo and Other Inconsequential Ramblings of a Condemned Man

I live my life in "The Bag."

The AH-64 Apache attack helicopter has a built-in night vision system. Attached to the nose of the aircraft, the Pilot Night Vision System/Target Acquisition and Designation System (PNVS/TADS) is approximately fourteen feet in front of the pilot's station and three feet below it. The system detects heat variances to create an image that is digitally projected onto a monocle in front of the pilot's right eye. The TV screen's field of view has a limited range of twenty degrees up and forty-five degrees down; however, if you look ninety degrees left or right, it can move at approximately 120 degrees per second. This is the PNVS. The TADS is comparable, though much slower. The system is "slaved" to the pilot's helmet electronically, so when you look left, the PNVS looks left.

My point is, everything you see is not originating from the location of your eye, but from fourteen feet in front of you and three feet below you. Your view is a hazy shade of green phosphorous, moving significantly slower than your head (taking time to catch up if you turn too quickly), and only shown through one eye. The effect can be nauseating.

So, they put you in The Bag during your initial training in the Apache. To make sure the visual cues you receive come only from the "Green-Eyed Monster" attached to your helmet–to ensure there is no competition between the PNVS view and the reality of what you see with your naked eye–your cockpit is sealed tight. Your visual system is all discombobulated and telling you one thing. Your vestibular system (your inner ear) is telling you something else. Your proprioceptive system (seat of your pants) is telling you a third story. Which do you believe?

The effect is nauseating–until you learn how to interpret your new world and read the new inputs.

This is life with MS. What your eyes tell you, what your sense of balance tells you, and what your seat-of-the-pants feeling tells you, often in direct conflict with reality. Nauseating—that may be the greatest understatement of my life. My new world is always changing.

In a helicopter, you are taught to rely on your instruments. Do not execute a maneuver simply because your body is telling you to do something. Rely on your instruments as your fourth sensory input.

What can I rely on with my body? When I stand up, what my eyes tell me (when my vision is clear and stationary) often conflicts with what my inner-ear balance tells me (when the signals work), as well as what my physical sensations tell me (when I can feel them). I have no instruments (at least not until Google develops a contact lens with a built-in attitude indicator, altimeter, and ground speed sensor). Nauseating, until I learn how to interpret my new world and read the ever-changing inputs.

Army aviation taught me how to function with MS. I have a new set of EMERGENCY PROCEDURES. I can't rely solely on one sensory input, I must use all of them. Sometimes, one of my sensors fails. I need to recognize that promptly, switch my focus from the failing sensor to my remaining sources, then LAND AS SOON AS PRACTICABLE (the primary concern is the urgency of the emergency).

When inputs across multiple sensors fail, LAND AS SOON AS POSSIBLE (the primary concern is survival of the occupant).

So, if we are out somewhere and I suddenly sit down or don't want to do anything, I apologize, but my primary concern may be survival of my occupancy.*

*This information is unclassified and, because I retired seventeen years ago, it is most likely outdated.

* * *

Dizziness and Vertigo: people with MS may feel off balance or lightheaded, or—much less often—have the sensation that they or their surroundings are spinning (vertigo).

XIII - Fatigue and Other Inconsequential Ramblings of a Condemned Man

Regarding fatigue, there has been a cycle throughout my life.

When I was a baby: just fall asleep, wherever, whenever.

When I was a child: just take a nap.

When I grew older: just go to bed early.

When I was in the Army: just SUCK IT UP, CUPCAKE!

After my army days: just don't go out tonight, go to bed early.

When Eleanor was born: just take a nap.

I long for the days when I was able to fall asleep, wherever, whenever. For now, I am in a constant state of limbo, fatigue.

When does fatigue set in? When does fatigue replace other words?

Tiredness?

Weariness?

Weakness?

Lethargy?

Laziness?

Fatigue is not only a battle with my MS, but it also leads to a struggle with every perception I face, with myself and others. Many of my symptoms have their telltale signs: a limp, struggling to use a fork, slurring and staggering, even my oddball forgetfulness. They are usually signs or indicators that "something is not quite right" with KB.

Sometimes, my fatigue is more than merely being tired. I may appear groggy and lethargic and look as if I have been awake for the last forty-seven hours; however, this is sometimes not the case. Sometimes, I have plenty of energy, but I just can't do anything with my body except sit there and watch TV, drink a beer with my friends, or stare at the computer.

Is it physical? Mental? Emotional?

Yes. Yes. Yes.

Fatigue is the loss or degradation of energy—physical, mental, and emotional. I track so many points of data every day, I've developed the ability to forecast fatigue. Fatigue occurs when I do any of the following:

- Don't get enough sleep (less than six hours for two or more days in a row).
- Get too much sleep (more than eight hours).
- Get too hot/too cold.
- Don't have enough sugar in my diet/too much sugar in my diet.
- Exercise too hard or too long/don't get enough exercise.
- Follow the same regimen for too many days in a row/have too much flux in my schedule.
- Push myself too hard/don't have enough activity in my day.

There are days when everything is perfect—when my sleep, diet, and exercise blend perfectly with the weather and with the external demands of life—but even on those rare, jewel-like moments, it's a fifty-fifty crapshoot as to whether I'm going to have the energy to do what I want or need to do.

I've never been middle-aged before. Maybe some of it has to do with my forty-five-year-old body. I don't know.

When Brie and I moved to Oregon, I fell in love with hiking and climbing. For me, nothing compared to the feeling of pushing my body up and down steep trails for hours, in peaceful solitude, with only my thoughts and music. The first few hikes absolutely kicked my ass within forty-five minutes. I thought it was just my Bronx-born body rejecting nature until a friend of mine recommended getting a set of trekking poles. Something so simple—removing the struggle of trying to keep my balance—made all the difference to my energy level. My speed increased by three times and my endurance felt limitless. With my MS, the added struggles of balance, strength, memory, coordination, and so many other issues take their toll on what I can do. As my activity decreases, my ability to push myself the next day decreases as well. The cycle feeds on itself.

About all I can commit to is that I will never use my fatigue as an excuse to avoid doing something. I will proudly proclaim the reason I am not participating: I don't like it, I don't like you, I have something better to do, I think it is stupid, I don't like...
(fill in the blank). If, for some reason, I don't explain why I'm not participating, it is not because I don't want to, but because my body can't do anything at all. At least not at that moment. I promise, though, when I can, I will. That is, unless I really don't like you (in which case I will tell you).

But for now, I'm off to the gym. My body feels like it has some energy for physical therapy. I hope it lasts beyond the drive there.

* * *

Fatigue occurs in about 80% of people with MS, can significantly interfere with the ability to function at home and work, and may be the most prominent symptom in a person who otherwise has minimal activity limitations.

XIV - Emotion, Depression and Other Inconsequential Ramblings of a Condemned Man

Finally, here is a topic about which I have zero concern! Yep, no problems here.

Thank you for reading.

Because you are still here, you already know me and are awaiting the punch line. Or possibly you're anticipating a juicy bombshell or two. Okay, here's one:

On several occasions, I completely lost the ability to manage and control the emotional effects of my MS. My condition has led to withdrawal, mood swings, irreparable damage to relationships, depression, and thoughts of suicide.

"Why would you admit such a thing?"

Good question (gold star for you!). There are so many reasons to come clean about my emotional fallibility.

First, my guess is that if you know me, this doesn't come as a surprise. Perhaps you recognize my predicament and feel sympathy for me. Maybe you just think I'm an asshole. I would like the opportunity to change your perception: no pity party, I'm not an ass (mostly). Second, if I constantly remind myself this condition exists, my awareness may be the tipping point to stave off catastrophic results in my next encounter. And third, if I share my story, hopefully someone out there will understand they are not alone in their fight. Because you are not alone.

I have repeatedly gone through a seemingly infinite loop of emotional changes. I fully expect to revisit each one in my long and prosperous future. The five stages of grief—denial, anger, bargaining, depression, and acceptance—are not restricted to just one pass-through. You experience them as often as you can endure. My first struggle lasted more than four years.

Denial

The shock of my initial diagnosis was softened by the fact that I could continue my assignment in the Army. For some unknown reason, my commanders approved my request to remain in command of my air cavalry troop in Korea. My leaders showed the greatest act of trust, faith, and confidence to allow me, a non-deployable soldier, to remain deployed overseas in command of troops. I worked hard to minimize the effects of my disability by charging full speed into my work (and alcohol). Nine months later, I chalked up my return to the States as "their greatest mistake" and never looked back. In my new life in the civilian world, work and alcohol remained by my side. Peppered throughout this stage were manic highs and lows while I struggled to find a better life.

Anger

Anger was my first response to the initial MS diagnosis. During that period, I moved seven times, across three states and three continents. After three-and-a-half years, I ended up crashing (literally) out of this anger stage, leaving a lot of shattered relationships and despair in my wake.

I was angry with my MS for all it had taken from me. The silliest thing I was bitter about was war; I believed MS stole my life in the military before 9/11. I'm ashamed to admit I marginalized the suffering and sacrifice of so many by referring to it as something I missed out on. This was in 2002 and 2003. I had yet to realize some of the fantastic accomplishments I proudly boast of today; had I an ounce of foresight, my bar tabs would have been much, much lower.

Peppered throughout this stage were more manic highs and lows as I struggled to find a better life.

Bargaining

It was around this time that I drafted my first suicide note. I wrote a list of logical reasons why life was unbearable and unfair, and on the other side, I listed my fears, my hopes, my dreams. I struggled to see how I could accomplish those dreams when faced with such burdens. MS and suicide occupied my every thought. I would have given anything, done anything, to understand how to move forward, and past this state. I ran to the only place I could think of: to my mommy, my sister, and my brother. I was willing to give up everything (although I felt as if I truly had nothing) if I could find an answer.

So, my sister took me in and I gave up fighting and running. I stopped struggling with manic mood swings.

Depression

For seven months, I tried to rebuild the life I had before MS, only to realize it was neither the life I wanted nor a life I was capable of achieving. Career searches, neurology appointments, and psychological counseling kept me only slightly on the right side of sanity.

Acceptance

"If I just get a job, I can get back on my feet."

"If I just get a girlfriend, I can get back on my feet."

"If I can just get back to my feet..."

I finally stopped searching for a fix and managed to find solace in what I had to offer and where I was, right at that point in my life. Only after volunteering at the VA hospital, where I witnessed true suffering, true sacrifice, true service, did I choose to focus on where I was and what I had, instead of where I could or should be if I hadn't gotten MS.

I remember thinking back then how grateful I was to have gone through these difficult stages of grief and loss before I met Brie and before Eleanor was born. But what I didn't know was that that first round through the stages of grief was only one of many such struggles (and also the most pronounced).

I have continued to struggle through the rounds of denial—anger—bargaining—depression—acceptance:

- Every hospitalization, and every setback caused by my MS.
- Approaching the age my father was when he killed himself (forty-three years and seventy-nine days).
- Going through the process of having my VA disability reclassified to "100% Total and Permanent."
- The death and disability of friends, family, and loved ones, and the realization that I am not far behind.

There will be so many more stages to face, as there is much grief yet to come. In between, there will also be an endless string of emotional windfalls and emotional challenges.

I accept that challenge, and I raise you one bit of sarcasm, courtesy of Eleanor.

"What do you call a puppy on a bicycle?"

"A puppy bicycle!"

Exactly.

* * *

Emotional Changes

Can be a reaction to the stresses of living with MS as well as the result of neurologic and immune changes. Significant depression, mood swings, irritability, and episodes of uncontrollable laughing and crying pose significant challenges for people with MS and their families.

Depression

Studies have suggested that clinical depression–the severest form of depression–is among the most common symptoms of MS. It is more common among people with MS than it is in the general population or in persons with many other chronic, disabling conditions.

XV - Consequences of the Inconsequential Ramblings of a Condemned Man

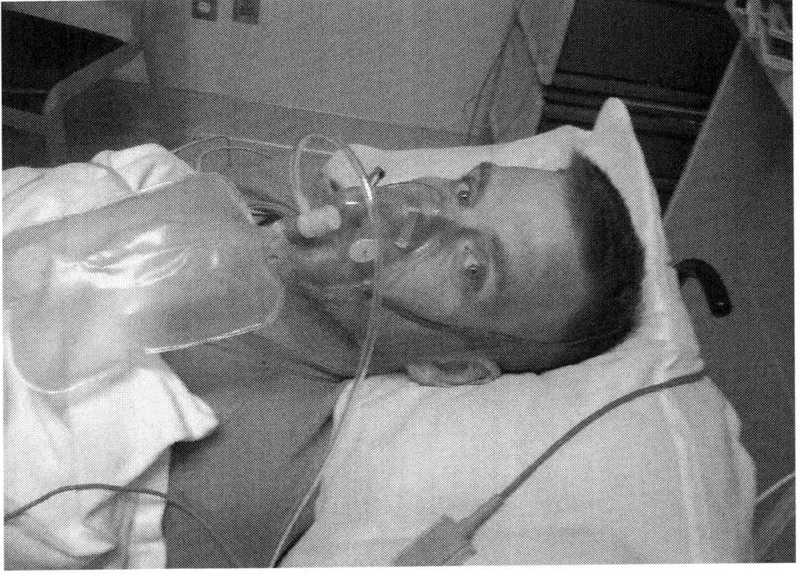

Complications, side effects, secondary and tertiary symptoms. Call them what you want, these consequences are the truly crippling effects of multiple sclerosis. My MS is not going to kill me; I can live a long, hindered life with numbness, pain, bladder problems, spasticity, etc. MS will not be the primary cause of my death. If all goes according to plan, when I die at the ripe old age of 109 years old, my MS will be but a side note.

If, however, and I'm just hypothesizing here, complications from multiple sclerosis do turn out to contribute to my premature demise, here's my top-five list of "MS Things That Are Probably Going to Kill Me."

5. I will suffocate or choke to death

I should have this down pat, as I choke on food and drink all day, every day. Choking is normally no cause for alarm because I carefully maintain a protocol, ensuring my clogged airway is cleared with minimal fuss or mess. This is, however, one of my less graceful moves. I will continue to find new ways to scare the hell out of myself at least once or twice a month. How many times can you play the lottery before you win?

4. I will die from a fall or have an accident

There are countless scenarios that fall under the general "accident" category. The usual suspects are everyday things such as driving, cooking, or swimming. I'm currently safe doing these and other activities, or I recognize my limits and steer clear, but I do understand my abilities will decline more than those of a "normal" aging man.

I'm a good driver, a safe driver–safer now than ever before. Nevertheless, I carefully watch and evaluate this one.

Brie, seeing how so many accidents occur in the kitchen, can I use this is as my excuse for wanting to eat out all the time instead of cooking?

I don't get into a pool or other body of water that's over my head; my comfort level in the one-arm-one-leg dog paddle is low.

Falling should be in a category of its own, separate from other accidents. While I'm cautious, I still fall regularly. This past winter, I fell and cracked my ribs getting out of the shower, then again shoveling ice and snow. A few years back, I suffered a dual spiral leg fracture while roller skating. Don't ask. It seemed like a good idea at the time. Now I have a titanium rod in my leg as a permanent reminder that it was not.

I still push myself because it is worth the risk to avoid becoming sedentary and then entirely immobile. I go beyond my limits regularly because I don't know where the moving bar is, or if my brain is ready to accept certain limitations. These days, I fall quite often, but without serious consequences. However, anything can change at any moment. Hopefully, I will recognize this before I regret it.

3. I will die of an infection

In 2007, I nearly lost my leg (and I could have lost more) when a reaction to my medication developed into a staph infection. Aspiration pneumonia, which can turn into an infection, is a constant concern because I regularly aspirate food and drink into my lungs. Even minor cuts and scrapes can sometimes become a problem. Because I don't see or feel them, and therefore don't tend to them properly, they can become infected.

2. I will die from a medication reaction

Reactions to and side effects from medications are common. Some can be serious while others are just annoying. There's preliminary evidence (and a phase-three trial currently underway), to support the benefits of high-dose biotin for the treatment of MS. Biotin, or vitamin B7, commonly taken as a hair and nail growth supplement, is usually taken in daily doses of twenty to forty-five micrograms. I'm currently taking three hundred milligrams daily—the equivalent of hundred milligrams thousand micrograms! As you can imagine, my hair and nails are fantastic!

Some of my medications cause nausea (take with food, take on an empty stomach).

Many of my injectable medications cause bruising and other site reactions.

I would love to know what the heck I am taking to give me such incredible and offensive gas!

Then, there are the bad reactions I've experienced: staph and other bacterial infections, gastrointestinal reactions, anaphylaxis, meningitis.

I am on an immunosuppressant, which reduces my body's natural immune system. I get it. Medications are one thing where the "Army Strong" mentality of "Give me what you've got, I can take it!" does not apply. I can't take it, so please give me only as much as I need.

1. I will kill myself

This is a hard thing to imagine and even harder to write. I honestly have no idea how far down the rabbit hole I went on my other trips, nor do I care to find out. I don't want this to happen and am shaken to the core just by discussing the topic of my suicide.

Suicide is a reality for everyone. For those at increased risk for suicide, for whatever reason, it will always be a danger, one that will not go away and must be acknowledged, confronted, and respected if it is going to remain suppressed.

If you are in need, if you are scared—reach out.

You are not alone.

* * *

The National MS Society is Here to Help

NEED MORE INFORMATION?

We Are Here

Our MS Navigators help identify solutions and provide access to the resources you are looking for. Call 1-800-344-4867 or contact us online.

NEWLY DIAGNOSED

If you or someone close to you has recently been diagnosed, access our MS information and resources.

XVI - Harsh Realities of the Inconsequential Ramblings of a Condemned Man

Right now, there is nothing on the market with the ability to cure my MS or send it into remission. It is debatable whether the medications I am current taking are slowing the progression of my MS and giving me more time. There is no known way to recover the functionality I have lost, or will lose, from the damaging effects of my MS. There is no way to predict, identify, or isolate early-onset MS, and eradicate the disease before it affects the next generation.

Not yet.

Overcoming these realities is my dream. The only possible way we are going to win this is with more research and development. Because it is a fight.

The fight is not over and it won't be over until a cure is found.

It will never stop...nor will we

It will never quit...nor will we

This is why we fight!

This is forever my pitch: to support our fight and share our message as far as your networks will take it. I first shared my beloved message of dedication and hope on April 30, 2008. At the time, I had no idea those words and my worsening condition would bring me to where I am today. But, where is that?

Am I on the launchpad or on the brink? I hope the answer is the former.

"Pray for the best, expect the worst, be prepared for both."

Over the course of writing these ramblings, I shared my soul (or showed my ass) in ways I never have before. When Brie read some things she hadn't known about me before, I wondered if I had gone too far. If I'm going to ask for support, you need to understand why. If I'm going to ask others to give what they can, I must demonstrate how I am giving everything I have.

"You have five minutes to win their hearts. Aaaaand, GO!"

Here are just a few examples.

If my MS is going to cripple me, it will have a formidable opponent. I will put up a fight.

I spend two to four hours a day in physical therapy, pushing my body to its limits. Most days, I fall short of what I could do in the past. Yesterday, I showed improvement in my strength and endurance. I hope to match that goal today. Baby steps...

It's not all bad. I do spend a lot of time on elliptical machines and stationary bikes, giving me time to binge-watch a multitude of TV series. By the end of next week, I will be free to converse with anyone interested in season five of *Arrow*! [Line forms here]

I will continue to adapt and overcome.

There is more than one way to skin a cat, so to speak.

When MS turned my already-childlike scribble into utterly illegible scratch, I started to type everything. As my ability to type on a keyboard diminished, I transitioned to voice-to-text software. Every blog post I "write" and even the book you are currently reading is, more accurately, "The Spoken Word of KB." (I expect a lecture from my priest for such blasphemy.)

I will demonstrate my tenacity and conviction in searching for a cure.

As part of a continued search for the right combinations of medications, I am currently on approved medication #9 and trial medication #2. I don't know when number ten or number three will become available.

I will continue to serve my community.

My efforts remain focused through various nonprofit organizations, within my church, and as part of our continuing effort to defeat MS. I will thrive as a loving father, husband, dog owner, as the K in EMBK, as a loving family member, neighbor, and friend.

And, I will do more.

My effort to drive support led to the founding of NEVER STOP NEVER QUIT, a nonprofit organization dedicated to augmenting the existing efforts to fight MS. Its mission is to raise funds, support treatment, and promote awareness in the fight against multiple sclerosis. One hundred percent of the net revenue generated by NEVER STOP NEVER QUIT will support larger national organizations, with the specific purpose of finding a cure for, and managing the devastating effects of, multiple sclerosis.

There is much more to come with this adventure. And I will do more, whether it is speaking at national and regional events, writing books, or selling motivational swag. Many efforts are currently being taken to continue raising awareness of and funding for our fight.

I will share my story with the world.

Remember, you are not alone.

I have so much more to say, so many more inconsequential ramblings. I still don't have personal experience with many of the devastating effects that MS rains down upon its victims. Unfortunately, though, I will. Some ramblings are not mine to experience alone. I share them with others fighting MS, our families, our friends, our caretakers. We'll figure out how to get there together.

And when I finally finish every one of the efforts I have undertaken, when there is nothing left that my body or mind can do, I'm confident that my one small contribution will be a glorious footnote in a featured article published in the *Official Journal of the American Academy of Neurology*, entitled, "Finally: The Key to Fighting MS Revealed."

How was that?

"Four minutes and fifty seconds. Not bad."

Oh! Then, Never Stop...Never Quit...!

XVII - Aftermath of the Inconsequential Ramblings of a Condemned Man

NEVER STOP NEVER QUIT!

WWW.NEVERSTOPNEVERQUIT.COM

I first completed my series of ramblings in June 2017. By November, so much was different (yet again).

For the past fifteen years, I have reached out to friends, family, and colleagues with one message: the fight is not over, and it won't be over until a cure is found.

My delivery of this belief has morphed over time.

2003 - I was strong then. At the time, I wrote:

> I want to show my thanks to those who helped me along the way. I want to fight for those who can't, and

ensure that our next generation will never hear the words, "You have MS."

2005

Every day, Brie and I deal with the effects of my MS. Fortunately, all of the treatments, aid, and support I have received since 1999, when I was first diagnosed, have helped. But it is a fight. The fight, however, is not over. For me, and for the 1,250 people with MS living in Delaware, it won't be over until a cure is found.

2007 – My words documented a declining but hopeful fight as my MS progressed.

My medical condition has stabilized (to a point). Though still somewhat debilitated, at least I am able to function day to day. I am under constant treatment at the Veterans Health Administration (VHA). I am "healthy" today because of the treatment and support they have given me. Physically, I am as stable as I can hope to be—until we find a cure.

2011

It has been eleven years now since I first heard those words, "You have MS." Like many others, my course is a daily struggle with the pain and damaging effects of the disease. I am able to fight back though! Because of the amazing medical treatment I receive from my doctors at the Veterans Affairs Hospital, my body is strong. Through the constant love and guidance from my friends and family, I have been able to maintain my daily routine. And, the support from advocacy groups like the National Multiple Sclerosis Society (NMSS) has kept me prepared for today—and for whatever may happen next!

2015

My arms and hands are failing, my voice is weak, my upright and mobile days are fading. My fight, however, remains strong. ***A World Free of MS*** is still our vision. The daily occurrence of new MS diagnoses reminds us that we don't yet have a cure. The rapid worsening of my own health is a constant reminder of the paramount challenges for all of us who are affected by MS.

> We will win this fight. My goals remain set on the recovery and rehab I'll need to be able to dance with my daughter, Eleanor, again. Even if I don't reach that target, I'll continue fighting to ensure that her generation never has to hear the words, "You have MS."

2017–???

As I look back on my tale of adversity and resilience, I see that there was a strikingly haunting tone—one of familiarity in the MS community. The steady progression of my disease is, unfortunately, all too common in those fighting with the disease for so long. I was sure that I would be the exception that proves we are on the verge of defeating MS. I didn't want to believe my course.

As summer wore on and the heat began causing serious health problems for me, the treasured motivational burst I normally experienced before, during, and right after Bike MS sputtered and stalled. Shortly after the ride, my condition worsened again. My leg weakened and my arm became less functional.

I grew restless from the seemingly futile efforts of generating motivation and fundraising for MS. I felt as if I was working toward a fictional future. Anxiety and depression kicked in, but I simply passed it off as a by-product of this highly stressful period in my life. But, hey, that's my specialty, right? I take pride in my ability to excel amidst such adversity.

This was too much. And, it had been going on for too long.

I Stopped

I stopped reaching out to fundraise, no longer focused on my fight to defeat MS. Instead, my energy switched to higher priorities: repairing issues in my personal life and focusing on writing about things other than MS. Unfortunately, I didn't make any headway in either OF those endeavors. I wasn't going anywhere; my fruitless efforts merely occupied the hours until each day would end. When I woke the next day, I started right where I left off: still in limbo.

My depressed state may have snuck up on me, but it did not go by unnoticed. By documenting my dilemma in my blog series, I attempted to confront my fears. Meeting face-to-face with—let's call it what it is—this huge mountain of shit, didn't have the effect I was hoping for. As I faced the complexities of my disease, I finally realized...they were not going away anytime soon.

I Quit

I didn't have much of a reaction as my world slowly crumbled around me. I didn't hit the bottle; in fact, any drinking decreased significantly. I didn't go out and further self-destruct. Instead, I didn't do much of anything, except hope for things to get better...somehow. I was idly waiting for my *deus ex machina.* My anxieties and fears increased when I accepted that there is no salvation primed and ready to go, and no more treatment options. A cure or effective treatment, if one exists yet, is still in the pipeline of research, discovery, development, manufacturing, and testing. My body and my mind must bear the burden of hanging on until our day comes.

This is where I remained for several months: in a perpetual cycle of increasing debilitation, anxiety, and depression. My symptoms were worsening. It was difficult to tell if my slide was medically induced or being fed by my depression. It was probably some combination of the two, but there's no way to know for sure. Neither factor was going away anytime soon.

The fight is not over and it won't be over until a cure is found.
It will never stop...nor will we
It will never quit...nor will we
This is why we fight!

As I watched the year's fundraising season come to a close, I sat by in amazement as the unthinkable played out, over and over.

I stopped reaching out and fundraising, yet our friends and loved ones continued to provide incredible support. Over $60,500 came in. Together, we propelled Eleanor to the rank of number one Bike MS fundraiser in Oregon for 2017!

I stopped recruiting riders and building support for Team Amulet, yet another incredible array of friends, both old and new, rallied to ride and celebrate. Together, as Team Amulet, we raised over $84,700 in 2017! Since its inception in 2003, Team Amulet has now raised more than $633,000!

Though I felt strangely alone, my friends, family, and loved ones rallied around our fight. Many found inspiration in my words. Eleanor and I were honored to be asked to speak and to celebrate with the NMSS Kentucky-Southeast Indiana Chapter. We appeared in promotional videos for the NMSS Oregon Chapter and for a national MS marketing campaign. I was praised for my great work and dedication many times over. While my own world continued to darken around me, I finally began to see the light so many others were generating in support of our fight.

I received a shocking reminder of something I had lost sight of long ago: The fight is not over and it won't be over until a cure is found.

It will never stop. My body and mind will stumble. There may be times when I will break, although hopefully I'll pick myself back up and start again soon, but the collective "We" will never stop.

It will never quit. While I face this gut-wrenching struggle to keep fighting and not give up, the collective "We" will never quit. I am not alone in this fight.

I can't even begin to express my love to all who helped carry me, even before I realized I was in need.

So now what?

That, my friends, is a question for which I would love to have an answer! I don't know. Even today, I'm still trying to formulate a response. My first step was to address some of the clutter clouding my mind and feeding my fears. Personal issues (divorce, moving, finances, etc.) were pounding on an already weakened body.

My next goal is to accept the fact that I am disabled. Simply fighting to discount my adversities is pointless; they are here for the long haul and will probably get worse.

If you haven't seen me in a year, my disability is far greater now.

If you haven't seen me in a month, my disability is worse now.

You haven't seen me in a week...

Every day, I need to learn how all of this affects my life from this day forward. There are no options when your body fails and functions are lost—you simply must learn a new way to live. That's what I must do. My first blog post of 2017 was 45 Is the New 0. I didn't realize how much worse everything would get, and in such a short time, but I guess my commitment still stood true.

Every day, I remind myself "It starts today."

I eliminated the distractions and switched my focus to my three priorities: my health, my mind, and My Little Love. Reducing the anxieties caught in my mind is surely a welcome remediation. I'll focus on serenity. I stepped away from my all-too-consuming social media distractions to get back to my writing.

I focused my attention on rehabilitative and medical efforts as well as on the logistical preparations for when my condition progresses beyond self-management.

Finally, I relished in renewed magic with My Little Love. Eleanor was finally at the age where the memories we make will last a lifetime. If my body only has a short window of opportunity, those memories will be fantastic.

The fight against MS is surely not over, nor is my personal battle. My "sabbatical" ended and, for me, it was time to share my words. Most of you who know me already realize I don't reach out very much, if at all. Writing is my escape—I share all my fears, concerns, joys, and imagination without having to open myself up at all (yes, I get the lunacy of my logic). I sincerely look forward to describing what this journey looks like when completed, and I prepare for the next adventure.

Until that day comes, please receive my sincere thanks for all the support you continue to give all of us fighting MS. We need every bit of it, and I apologize for not saying "thank you" enough.

Love,

Kevin

The fight is not over and it won't be over until a cure is found.

It will never stop...nor will we

It will never quit...nor will we

This is why we fight!

Never Stop...Never Quit...

Please support our fight –

Main.NationalMSSociety.org/goto/EMBK

About the Author

Kevin was born and raised in New York City. A graduate of the United States Military Academy at West Point, he was diagnosed with multiple sclerosis (MS) in 1999, while serving overseas in command of a US Army Air Cavalry Troop. He is now medically retired and lives in Portland, Oregon with his daughter, Eleanor.

Kevin devotes much of his time and energy towards overcoming the challenges of his own MS, so he can fight for others. He began writing and blogging in 2010, for the Department of Veterans Affairs, the National MS Society, and then NEVER STOP NEVER QUIT, a charitable foundation he co-formed to further expand his fundraising and advocacy in the fight against MS.

"...fantastic stories, where I'm limited only by my imagination, not by the confines of this stupid disease."

NMSS Leadership Conference
Denver, CO
November 2016

Copyright

Published 2018 by
NEVER STOP NEVER QUIT, Portland, OR
NeverStopNeverQuit.com

ISBN: 978-1-7324106-0-2

79401774R00210

Made in the USA
San Bernardino, CA
16 June 2018